BIRTHDAY BOYFRIEND

Quinn Valley Ranch, Book 4

LIZ ISAACSON

ISBN-13: 978-1638761266

CHAPTER ONE

"Granny?" Jessica Quinn pushed open the front door of her grandmother's cottage at the same time she called her name.

The house smelled delicious, like salted cured meats and yeast—which could only mean one thing. Kolaches.

Her granny was famous for her sausage kolaches, and Jessie could only hope she could eat one now *and* at poker night later.

"Betsy said you'd have something for me tonight," she said, feeling weary from head to toe. Perhaps she shouldn't have agreed to take her sister's place at the monthly poker night.

Betsy usually played the cards with a few cowboys here at Quinn Valley Ranch, but since she and Knox had become more serious, she'd been getting subs for her poker games. Jessie had said no a couple of times now, because she knew who Betsy played with.

And she didn't need to make a bigger fool of herself in front of Flynn Hollister. The man was her brother's right-hand-man and most trusted cowboy. And a complete player.

Well, not really, but he sure did have a lot of ladies falling all over him all the time.

"Hello, dear," Granny said as she turned from the stove. She'd been brushing an egg wash on a sheet pan of unbaked kolaches, and they were the most beautiful sight Jessie had ever seen. "I'm running a bit behind. Can I bring these down to you when they're done?"

"Oh, you don't have to do that," Jessie said. "I can swing back this way and get them."

"Pish posh," Granny said. "I'll do it. Betsy said you just needed them by seven."

Honestly, Jessie had no idea what time it was. She needed a shower and a nap, and she could only have one at the expense of the other. "Yeah," she said.

"So I'll bring them down. You go ahead and go get yourself all dolled up."

Jessie laughed and took a foil-wrapped chocolate from the bowl on Granny's counter. Her grandmother always had something good to eat in that bowl, and Jessie really needed a sweet right now.

"It's nothing to get dolled up for," she told Granny.

"Betsy said there would be cowboys there." Granny smiled at her, those bright blue eyes sparkling with mischief. Jessie had seen this look before, and she didn't like it. Not one little bit.

"Yeah, Granny," she said dryly. "All the same cowboys I see around the ranch every day." She shook her head. "Trust me, no one to impress."

"Oh, there's someone," Granny said as if she could work magic and produce a cowboy that would look at Jessie and see the woman she was. "You just listen to Granny and go get ready. I'll bring these by later."

Jessie took another chocolate as she chuckled. "All right,

Grams. Thanks so much." On her way out the front door, she sent a quick message to Betsy.

You owe Granny. Did you know she's making kolaches?

She said she wanted to, Betsy sent back. *Said it was a special night for you, and you needed the power of the Quinn kolaches.*

Jessie had no idea what that meant, but she knew Granny had a funny way of trying to set up her grandchildren. This couldn't be that—it was only kolaches. And Betsy brought food to all the poker games.

Bringing something to share was part of the rules. Everyone looked forward to Betsy's culinary creations, so they'd already be disappointed when Jessie walked in instead of her sister. Thankfully, Jessie would have the kolaches, and she suddenly wondered if they did hold some power she didn't know about.

Once at the homestead, Jessie showered and shaved her legs and then got busy curling her hair in the basement bathroom, hoping with everything she had that Cami wouldn't come downstairs. Then she wouldn't have to explain anything to her little sister.

She could sneak out the glass doors down here, and no one would have to know she'd dolled herself up as if she were going to church to go to...poker night out in the east barn.

Flynn hadn't had a girlfriend for about a week now, and Jessie thought tonight was as good of a night as any to show him he didn't have to go into the dance hall to find his next date. She was right there in front of him, working alongside him every day out on the ranch.

Not that Flynn ever had to look very hard for a willing female to hold his hand or spend time at his side.

"It's no wonder," Jessie muttered to herself as she swept mascara on her eyelashes. The man was drop-dead gorgeous, and she may or may not have had a huge crush on him for the past year.

And he was so *Flynn* that he hadn't even noticed her attempts at flirting. Or she was just really bad at it. Either way, she hadn't been on a date in a really long time. Most men slid their attention right past her to Cami, the more feminine sister, the one with more blonde in her hair than red, the one who wore pumps while Jessie wore cowgirl boots.

Grabbing her phone, she quickly texted Betsy. *You didn't tell them I was coming, did you?*

Of course not, Betsy sent back. *If I had, they'd all cancel.*

Jessie frowned at the message, not sure if she should take it as a compliment or not. It wasn't her fault she was extraordinarily gifted at games, especially card games that required her to read another person.

It also wasn't her fault she worked her father's ranch with her brother and all the cowboys so that she had better biceps than most women. She'd learned, though, that a lot of men found her intimidating, and she attributed that to her lack of male interest.

And Granny said she brought over the kolaches. They're sitting on the upstairs kitchen counter.

Jessie groaned, because now she had to go upstairs. Cami would surely see her then, and she'd be late to poker night. She didn't want to be late. She actually wanted to be early, so she could lean against the chicken coop in the distance and watch Flynn enter the barn.

She pushed the thought away. She wasn't a creeper. She just had a crush. *An insane crush,* she told herself, as Flynn had always viewed her and treated her like a little sister. And yet, the hope inside her wailed with strength, and she hadn't been able to let go of the fantasy of the two of them together.

After glossing her lips with a wand of peach delight, she pulled on her cowgirl boots and checked her T-shirt. It wasn't as manly as the plaid shirts she wore to work in, and she'd decided she could try to make Flynn realize she was a woman and not just another one of the guys. The pink shirt clung to her curves and the word COWGIRL was spelled out in black letters across her chest.

He could read, she knew that. She wondered if he'd even look at her at all tonight. Invisibility seemed to be another of Jessie's specialties, and she actually prayed for the superpower as she crept upstairs to get the snack Granny had left for her.

"Still warm," she said around the sweet dough and spicy sausage. She'd just turned to escape out the back door when Cami came through it. She paused, taking in Jessie's curled hair and sliding her eyes down to her best cowgirl boots.

"Where are you going?" Her eyes widened as she pulled in a breath. "Oh, my stars. Do you have a date?"

Not yet, she thought as she scoffed for her sister's benefit. "No, of course not. Poker night."

Cami's eyes narrowed. "Poker night? You look like you're going out with the hottest man in town." She reached out and gripped Jessie's forearm. "Just tell me who he is."

"He's no one," Jessie said, already frustrated with the questions. Betsy, Cami, and Georgia had been trying to get Jessie to say who she had a crush on for months now. It wasn't happening. The Quinns weren't exactly known for their secret-keeping abilities, and while she loved her sisters, she didn't trust that one of them wouldn't accidentally say something to someone.

And before she knew it, Flynn would know about her crush and she'd never get the opportunity to go out with him.

She looked down at the kolaches, actually praying for whatever power Granny thought they had. "I'm going to be late," she said. "Don't wait up for me."

"Hey, just a sec," Cami said as Jessie breezed by her. "Mom wanted me to double-check and make sure you're free tomorrow night."

"For what?"

"For your birthday," Cami said, shaking her head as she smiled. "I swear, Jess, you're the only person who doesn't remember their own birthday."

"I am not," she said, though she couldn't say she was overly excited about turning thirty. Maybe if she had a boyfriend to kiss her and bring her flowers, sure. But tomorrow would just be another day, with calves to feed and hay to mow and Flynn to admire. "Tomorrow's fine," she said.

"No hot dates?"

"Nope," she said, escaping out the door and practically flying down the steps to the blue and white ranch truck she used. She didn't actually own her own car. Or a house. Or much of anything.

When Rhodes took over the ranch, he'd move from the cabin beside Gramps and Granny to the homestead. She and Cami still lived there, and so would Betsy and Georgia until they got married and moved out. She wasn't entirely sure of their plans, but she knew Rhodes would let her stay in the homestead as long as she wanted.

Honestly, she wanted to just trade places with him. He could have the homestead; she'd take his cabin.

Her heart started beating faster and faster the closer she got to the east barn. By the time she got out of the truck and collected the tray of kolaches, her pulse sprinted through her chest. She managed to walk to the doors and open them to find the atmosphere lively and charged, with a round table set up for poker and a long one holding the food.

"Jessie?" Newt asked, and it was as if everything came screeching to a halt. All the conversation. All the laughter. All the eating.

"Hello, boys," she said, adding a sway to her hips as she walked toward the food table. "Betsy needed a sub, and so here I am."

A collective groan went up, but Jessie just smiled around at each of them. Newt. Clay. Wyatt.

And Flynn.

Her heartbeat fluttered now, especially when he stepped forward and asked, "Are these the famous Quinn kolaches?"

"Mm hmm," she said, taking in a deep breath of that sexy cologne and trying not to swoon at his nearness. His dark eyes looked from the tray of food she carried to her eyes, and she dove right on in and started swimming around.

It was dangerous in those depths, but she didn't care.

Tonight, she felt lucky.

After all, she had the kolaches—and all of Flynn Hollister's attention.

CHAPTER TWO

Flynn Hollister's mouth had gone dry the moment the redhead had entered the barn. Jessica Quinn.

She already had half of his heart and she didn't even know it. He had mad respect for the woman, as she could hold her own against any problem on the ranch. She remembered little things, like birthdays and anniversaries, someone's favorite color or favorite treat. And she had legs that went on for miles and knew exactly how to wear a pair of jeans.

He'd just sworn to Rhodes that he was going to complete a thirty-day female fast, so Jessie was off-limits. Of course, she'd been forbidden for the past five years, as she was the boss's daughter and his best friend's little sister.

She turned and put the tray of kolaches on the table, twisting back to him with a flirty smile. Oh, so she was going to be Fun Jess tonight. Flynn forgot his own name for a moment, especially when he looked down at her shirt.

Cowgirl screamed back at him, and he let his eyes travel down her body to those boots. Heat boiled in his stomach, and he cleared his throat and looked away. No one seemed to notice the interaction between him and Jessie.

No, Newt, Clay, and Wyatt had formed a huddle, no doubt trying to scheme how they could combine their knowledge to beat Jessie. They didn't play for real money out in the east barn, but no one wanted to be humiliated.

"Doing something fun for your birthday tomorrow?" Flynn asked, putting his eyes on the food, which was much less dangerous than Rhodes's sister.

His *sister*.

Flynn's stomach flipped. His best friend and boss would not approve of Flynn even *looking* at Jessie wrong. And the things he thought about...he was taking those to the grave. He'd learned that a lot of things could be kept secret until death, as he'd endured losing his father and his farm in the same week.

The loss still stung five years later, and he picked up a handful of the honey mustard pretzels Wyatt had brought. Food had never been an adequate distraction for Flynn. Sometimes work was. Dating and dancing did nicely—at least until it was time to go home.

Flynn hated going home alone, but he wasn't stupid. He didn't sleep around, and he didn't kiss and tell, and he didn't have anything to be ashamed about. He couldn't help it if the women liked the way he looked. Liked that he was the best dancer in town. Liked his cowboy hat.

The problem was, none of them liked what was behind those things. A twinge of longing made his heart squirm, and Jess still hadn't answered his question.

He looked at her to find her dark, hazel-green eyes on him too. "Turning thirty, I think," he added, trying to get the conversation going. The other guys would just throw her daggered looks all night as she won game after game. Flynn would be frustrated too—and completely amused and even more attracted to her because of her skills at the poker table.

In fact, there wasn't anything Jess couldn't do, and while

that scared him a little, he kind of wanted to saddle up and see how far she could go.

"Yes," she finally said. "No big plans."

"Maybe you and I should do something to celebrate," he said, unsure of where the words had come from.

"Flynn," Clay said, causing him to turn away from the surprised look on Jess's face. "Jessie. Let's go. Time to start."

Jessie turned around and took a plate from the stack, tucking that beautiful hair behind her ear as she contemplated the spread before her. It was mostly packaged food, though Newt had brought his mother's fresh salsa. She took some of that and started loading her plate with chips as Flynn walked away, a fantasy of kissing her spicy lips later.

Of course, he would not be doing that. Not even close.

You're on a female fast, he reminded himself as he analyzed the seating arrangements at the table. Sitting right next to Jess would be best, but it seemed every man wanted to do that. Sitting across from her also gave Flynn a thrill, because he'd be able to stare at her without censoring himself.

After all, he had to be able to read the woman as they played. Boots shuffled, and Flynn finally sat down. Wyatt sat next to him, and Clay dove for the seat on the other side of Flynn, saying, "Jessie, you can sit by me."

"All right," she said, still at the table with all the food.

Flynn rolled his eyes as Clay smiled real big. "She's going to kill us," he said. "No matter where we sit."

"It's just Skittles," Clay said, as if he didn't mind being trampled during their poker night. He did, Flynn knew. He did too, but if there was anyone he wanted to completely trounce him, it was Jess. She made him feel like he was winning when he was losing.

His thoughts wandered straight back five years, to the last serious girlfriend he'd had. Sandra had been his everything, and she'd broken his heart exactly two weeks before his father had died.

Flynn had emerged from those tragedies a completely different person. Without a farm to work, he'd come to Quinn Valley Ranch, because he'd grown up with Rhodes and they'd stayed friends as they moved into adulthood.

"Who's dealing?" Newt asked, and Flynn handed him the deck of cards. Newt looked at him. "I don't want to deal first."

"I'll deal first," Jessie said, taking her place directly across from Flynn. Their eyes met, and he swore the temperature in the barn went up twenty degrees. Maybe thirty. She could achieve some serious smolder with those eyes, especially when she wore makeup the way she did tonight.

She lifted an oatmeal cookie to her lips, and Flynn almost moaned.

"Great," Newt said, reminding him he wasn't alone with her. "You deal first." He passed the cards to Wyatt, who set them in front of Jessie while she dusted cookie crumbs from her fingers.

She picked up the deck, and Flynn's heart skipped a beat. Now things were going to get interesting. He couldn't help grinning at her, and dang if she didn't give him a sexy little smile back.

Maybe he could date her. Just a little bit. No one had to know.

But you'll know, he told himself. And Jess didn't deserve to be with someone like him. She didn't deserve to be wined and dined and dumped.

And Flynn wasn't capable of committing to more than that. So he put on his poker face, and said, "Deal us in, Jess."

❅

A COUPLE OF HOURS LATER, JESSIE HAD INDEED WON nearly every hand. The two Clay managed to win were caught in the rafters of the barn, as the man had whooped so loudly the sound had gotten trapped there.

Flynn had won one hand. Newt, zero. Wyatt, zero.

Everyone filed out of the barn with the remains of their food, but Flynn hung back, slowly putting up their chairs and folding the table.

His heart seemed to be thumping out the words Female fast. Fe-male fast. Fe-fe-male fast. His brain matched the rhythm, leaving room for little else in his mind.

Jessie was so beautiful, though, and he couldn't help going over to her. "Need help?"

"I've got it," she said, glancing at him. Her hair fell between them, and Flynn wanted to push it back so badly.

Stop flirting with her, Flynn, and play your cards.

Clay had been particularly aggressive tonight. And fine, he had been flirting shamelessly with Jessie, thinking it might throw her off her game a little. At least that was what he'd told the other guys.

I'm not flirting. This is called strategy.

And he'd watched Jessie's face fall, each word exemplifying the kind of man Flynn was, and why she deserved so much better than him.

Still, he couldn't help pushing back that hair....

"Hey," he said. "You should be happier than you are. You won every hand."

"You won once," she said.

"Yeah, *once.*" He smiled at her, almost desperate to make her happy, see that smile.

"Why don't you live on the ranch with the other cowboys?" she asked.

Surprise flitted through Flynn. "I have a place in town."

He drew in a breath, wanting to be real with her. Tell her things no one but Rhodes knew. "When my dad died, I got a small inheritance. I, uh." He cleared his throat, this being-real thing so much harder than just laughing and dancing his weekends away. "I didn't want to be a cowboy on someone else's ranch, at least not in every way. So I bought my own place."

She looked at him, those eyes downright dangerous to his health. "I'm sorry about your dad."

"Yeah." He looked away. "I miss him almost every day." And not just because his mother had sold the farm Flynn had thought he'd work and then pass to his son in order to stay afloat financially.

"I bet." She picked up her tray of kolaches, and Flynn started taking down the table where the food had been.

"Listen," he said while he made quick work of putting the table away. "I meant what I said earlier." He turned and tucked his hands in his pockets. "About us going out."

"Oh." Her eyes filled with fire, and she took a step closer to him. "I don't know about that, Flynn."

"What don't you know about it?" He might as well hear what she had to say.

"Well, don't take this the wrong way, but I'm not really the flavor-of-the-week type of girl."

She wasn't a girl at all, and that T-shirt and those jeans testified of it. He nodded, her words worming their way all the way down into his gut, where they writhed. "Fair enough." He started toward her, expecting her to move out of the way or fall in step beside him.

She didn't do either of those, instead actually moving to block his escape. "You're...why do you do that?"

"Do what?"

"Come on," she said, frustration filling her expression now. Her mouth tightened, and dang if Flynn didn't want to kiss it until she relaxed into his arms. "Never mind. Not my—"

"I'm lonely," he blurted.

Their eyes met and held, and he could see Jessie was downright lonely too. He swallowed. "And I know I look good on the outside. I have some skills on the dance floor. And so I'm less lonely when I'm there, doing those things." He shook his head, in complete disbelief that he'd told her any of this.

"But women don't like what they find beneath the surface." He lifted his chin, almost daring her to contradict him. "So it's easier to cut them loose before they break up with me." Flynn stepped around her and headed for the door, humiliation burning through his bloodstream. The air outside held a crispness, though summer would fully arrive soon enough.

He drew in a deep breath and said over his shoulder, "It would be great if you could keep all that between us." He stepped into the night, almost desperate for her to join him, if only because he didn't want to leave her out here in the east barn by herself.

She's your best friend's little sister, he told himself. *Not your next girlfriend.*

"You comin'?" he called, and she flipped off the light in the barn and closed the door behind her. She'd parked next to him, and those long, delicious legs ate up the distance between them quickly.

She's the boss's daughter.

And yet, she stepped right over to him. "I know who you are inside," she whispered. "And maybe if you showed him on the outside, you'd have better luck with women."

He had no idea what to say, and it didn't matter anyway. She moved away from him as quickly as she'd come, put the nearly empty tray in her truck, and climbed in after it. She didn't look at him again, and she obviously wasn't as worried about leaving him out here as he'd been about driving off and leaving her alone.

Flynn watched her go, his heart thumping in his chest. *I know who you are inside.*

And of course, if anyone did, it would be Jess.

Still didn't mean he could actually go out with her.

CHAPTER THREE

essie couldn't believe what she'd said to Flynn. They'd always gotten along so well, and if they ever disagreed, he'd text her a few seconds after they parted ways.

He didn't do that tonight, and Jessie tossed and turned for what felt like hours before she finally fell asleep. She woke early in the summer, because her internal clock seemed to be timed to the sun.

Her day started with the calves, who would be going to auction in the fall. She kept immaculate records and made sure the cattle were properly immunized and healthy so they'd fetch the best price.

Flynn knew where to find her, but he didn't come. He'd surely arrived on the ranch already, and Jessie was so tired of thinking about him. But they'd flirted shamelessly during the poker game last night, and he'd blatantly asked her out.

"You blew it," she muttered to herself as the door to the barn opened. Her heart stuttered, thinking it would be Flynn. But it was Betsy, Georgia, Cami, and Rhodes, and they each carried a flaming cupcake.

She grinned at them as they began singing happy birthday to her. She used both hands to conduct them in the final strains of the song, and they all started laughing when it ended.

"Thank you, guys," Jessie said, watching as they put the cupcakes on the railing. She blew them out, refusing to make a wish about Flynn.

The man needed to open his eyes. Maybe she could wish for that.

She accepted a hug from all of her siblings, grinning as they all laughed together. "Happy birthday, Jess," Cami said, and everyone else said it too.

"We love you," Rhodes said.

"Dinner tonight," Betsy reminded her. "There will be a whole cake."

"Oh, I don't need a whole cake," Jessie said.

"Don't work too hard today," Georgia said. "Let's go get pedicures before your party." She raised her eyebrows. "What do you think?"

Jessie thought about what waited for her on her to-do list. She didn't want to do any of it. "Yeah," she said. "Let's do that."

"I'm in," Cami said.

"Me too," Betsy said.

"I'm out," Rhodes said with a laugh. "You girls have fun." He headed for the door. "I have to get back to work."

If there was someone who worked more than Jessie, it was Rhodes. And probably Flynn, as much as Jessie didn't want to admit it.

Everything came back to Flynn, and she really needed to figure out how to move past him. As her siblings left the barn, she tipped her head back and stretched her back at the same time she prayed.

"Please," she whispered. "Help me find a way to stop thinking about him."

She sighed, and she turned back to the cupcakes, one of which still smoked. Maybe she should leave the ranch. Find another job. She had an animal science degree, and she could be useful on another farm, another ranch, in another state.

Somewhere Flynn Hollister didn't live, so she wouldn't have to see him every day and wish she were different. Wish she were pretty enough to attract his attention. Wish she were someone he might be interested in.

The barn door opened again, and Jessie kept her back to it so she could have an extra moment to collect her emotions. She hadn't started crying yet, but the tears were so close, so close.

"Happy birthday, Jess," Flynn said, and she pulled in a breath that sounded like a gasp.

She glanced over her shoulder, barely looking at him. "Thanks."

He joined her in front of the four cupcakes her brother and sisters had brought. "Look, I—"

Jessie really wanted to hear what he was going to say. How he could explain away his invitation to go out, how she couldn't possibly know the real him because he didn't show it to anyone.

In the silence, she nudged a cupcake toward him and said, "Betsy made them. It'll be delicious."

A soft chuckle met her ears, and he picked up the treat and peeled off the paper. They ate together, and she found she just wanted him to leave. Being with him like this was too hard. He was too vulnerable, and she felt like he was torturing her on purpose.

He had to know how she felt about him. He simply *had* to, and he was so cruel not to do anything about it.

"Jess," he said, and she hated that he got to use such a personal nickname. Hated it and loved it.

"I've been an idiot," he said quietly. "Real stupid, especially when it comes to you."

"I don't know what you mean," she said, refusing to look at him. One glance at that rugged face, those beautiful eyes, and she'd forget she was mad at him.

He slipped his fingers between hers. "I'm sure you do."

Tears pricked the backs of her eyes, and she breathed in slowly, trying to stop herself from crying. She started mentally spelling out the names of the medications she used with the cattle, because that helped her focus on something besides the sparks moving through her bloodstream, and the warmth of Flynn's hand in hers.

"I like you, Jess," he said. "But you have to know why I haven't ever done anything about it."

"I know why," she said. "You always have a girlfriend."

A defeated sound came out of his mouth. "You're kidding."

"I wish," she said, thinking of all those girls and wondering how many he'd kissed. She shook her head and pulled her hand away. "It's fine, Flynn. It's—"

"Not fine," he said. "You're my best friend's little sister. Rhodes won't be happy about us going out." He moved around the post to the other side of the railing, leaving her no choice but to look at him.

Sure enough, he wore that adorable vulnerability in his eyes, and she had no defense against him.

"I like you, Jess," he said again. "You really are the only person who knows who I am, and somehow, I think you still like me too."

She couldn't deny it, but she didn't have to confirm it either. She simply stared at him, unblinking.

"You're my boss's daughter," he said next. "You have two

strikes against you, and I...I need this job. This ranch saved me, and I couldn't act on how I felt."

Felt.

Past tense.

Confusion swirled through her. "Okay," she said, nodding. Anything to end this conversation. "Thanks for stopping by."

"Jess."

"Why are you doing this to me?" she asked, her voice pitching up with every word. "It's fine, Flynn. I'm fine. You like me, I like you, we can't be together for some stupid reasons I don't understand. Whatever." The redhead in her emerged, and her fingers fisted. "Just go. This is torture."

He shook his head, his jaw clenching. "I'm not going. I came to tell you I don't care if Rhodes is upset, and I don't care if I get fired. I want to go out with you."

She gave a somewhat maniacal laugh. "We can't go out."

"Then we stay in," he said, taking her fisted fingers and uncurling them. He lifted her hand to his lips and gave her the sweetest kiss.

Everything inside Jessie felt like it was coming apart. She had very little composure left, and she just wanted him to go. Or maybe stay. She wasn't sure.

"Maybe we just see each other in secret for a while," he said, leaning his forehead against hers.

Jessie was finally able to get a full breath, and it shuddered on the way out. "Okay," she said, needing this situation to be lightened. "But I still want a birthday present from you. You'll come to my party tonight?"

"It's a family thing, right?" he asked, tracing the tip of his nose down the side of her face.

She leaned into his touch, revealing way too much about how she felt about him. "Yes," she said.

"I've come to stuff like that before, so I think I can swing it."

"Great," she said. "You can bring your present then."

"Sweetheart, *I'm* the present."

She giggled, enjoying standing in his arms. "Yeah? Are you my birthday boyfriend? Is that it?"

"If you want me to be," he said seriously, and Jessie pulled back and looked into his eyes. "Is that what you want for your birthday?"

He was what she'd wanted forever. Had wanted for so long. She felt like she was hallucinating, and all she could do was nod.

"Done." He pressed his lips to her cheek, backed up, and walked out of the barn.

"I WANT PINK," JESSIE SAID. "THE PEARLESCENT ONE, SINCE one of the June birthstones is pearl."

Georgia handed her the bottle of nail polish she'd pointed to. "What color should I get?"

"Red," Betsy said. "Like that barn where you and Logan fell in love."

"Oh, jeez," Georgia said, though she laughed a little. "So that means you'll be getting what? Pink too, because you and Knox fell in love on Valentine's Day?" She turned to Cami, who studied the array of polishes like they held the secret to world peace.

"No, wait," Georgia said. "Red, like the fiery depths of the bellows."

Betsy rolled her eyes. "Neither of those."

"Black," Georgia said. "The color of deception."

"That would be you," Betsy said.

"Please. You snuck around with Knox forever behind all of our backs."

Jessie stayed silent, letting her two older sisters have it

out. She wasn't about to say anything about her and Flynn's conversation that morning. Not now, anyway.

"Can you two stop?" Cami asked, glancing around the nail salon. "You both have boyfriends, and we don't. So just pick a color and let's do this." She glared at Georgia and Betsy, but Jessie was secretly glad.

Because now her sisters would pester Cami with questions. Sure enough, Betsy plucked a blue bottle of nail polish off the shelf, and said, "Cami, I thought you were dating Roger."

"Roger is a loser," she said through tight teeth.

Jessie exchanged a look with Georgia and Betsy. "Tell us what happened," Jessie said, following the nail technician to a massage chair. Cami had no problem talking about her feelings, and Jessie had no problem asking more leading questions so that Cami wouldn't stop.

After all, she could listen to her sister and daydream about Flynn at the same time.

CHAPTER FOUR

Flynn spent the afternoon agonizing over Jess's birthday party. He'd attended family things in the past, so his presence wouldn't be that big of a deal. He'd shake her father's hand and hug her mother, sit down to eat beside her grandparents. He'd done it all many times in the past, usually as Rhodes's guest.

But that didn't mean he couldn't show up tonight. Jess had invited him.

"You should tell him," he told himself as he worked on getting fresh water to every animal. The summer heat was brutal, and water was essential to life. But he couldn't tell Rhodes about Jessie—and not only because it was his little sister.

He'd pledged to a thirty-day female fast, and it had barely been a week.

Still stewing about Rhodes and the party and Jessie and how he really felt about her, he finished his work for the day and hurried home. He had to shower and put on fresh jeans to show up at the Quinns—at least if he wanted to be Jessie's birthday boyfriend.

And surprisingly, he did.

Flynn hadn't wanted to be anyone's boyfriend for a long time. Sure, women called him that. He went out with a few for longer than a few weeks. None longer than a few months.

His heartbeat bounced over itself as he drove to the florist and picked up a bouquet of flowers with carnations, roses, and a few more varieties he couldn't name.

They were neutral, exactly the type of thing he'd show up and give to a friend. His boss's daughter. A family thing.

But Flynn's thoughts about Jess didn't linger on her being like his sister. Oh, no. He'd always found her beautiful—striking really—but completely off-limits.

And out of his league.

She'd never acted like she was better than him, though she clearly was. He'd been so broken when he started at Quinn Valley Ranch, and she'd never treated him like that. He'd appreciated that, and as time went on and he moved through women, she'd never said one thing to him about it.

He pulled up to the homestead, where several cars and trucks had parked. The front door stood open, likely letting in the evening breeze through the screen door. His nerves crackled as he approached, the flowers gripped in one hand and his gift in the other.

No one greeted him at the door, and he went in without knocking. He was a few minutes late, but they obviously hadn't started yet. Her birthday cake sat on the counter in the kitchen, and Betsy bent over the oven to pull something out.

"Pizza's ready," she said. "Let's call everyone over, Jessie."

She turned around, saying, "C'mon, everyone. Time to eat." Her eyes landed on Flynn, and everything narrowed between them. He had the wherewithal to lift his hand to his hat to acknowledge her, but he hung back as the rest of her family got up from the living room and came over to the kitchen area.

"Hey," Rhodes said. "You made it."

"Yeah," Flynn said, glad his voice didn't sound as choked up as he felt.

Her father said grace, and after everyone had chorused, "Amen," he added, "And happy thirtieth birthday to our little girl." He swept Jess into a tight hug, where she laughed as the others said happy birthday.

"We'll do cake later," Betsy said. "Jessie wanted pizza, and we have pizza."

Flynn waited while the others got in line, glad when Jess came over to him. "Hey," he said, extending the flowers to her. "I got these for you."

"They're beautiful." She took them from him with a smile. "Thanks, Flynn."

"Happy birthday, Jess." He'd said it this morning, too, but he really wanted her to have an amazing birthday. "Is there a place for presents?"

She eyed the brown box he hadn't even wrapped. "I know what that is."

"Do you?" He felt flirtatious and playful, but he tried to tame it. He hid the box behind his back. "What is it?"

"I'm hoping it's a candle from Scentiments."

He chuckled and shook his head. "A man can't even surprise you." He handed her the box. "I know you like citrus scents, so it's a lemon and pink grapefruit one."

Her eyes burned into his, and she whispered, "I'd hug you if we were alone."

"Next time we are, then," he quipped.

She ducked her head, took her flowers and her candle over to the kitchen, and started arranging the blooms in a vase.

Flynn got in line, determined not to give anyone in her

family anything to talk about. He piled his plate with pizza and salad and sat at the end of the table near Rhodes.

"How's your mother, dear?" Charity asked, and Flynn looked at Rhodes's mother.

"She's okay, ma'am." Flynn smiled at the woman who'd been a second mother to him his whole life. "I get up to Lewiston to see her as often as I can."

"And how's Widow Jones?"

"Oh, she's already complaining about the heat." Flynn chuckled. "I checked on her air conditioner, and it's working fine."

"She just loves having something to complain about," Gertrude said from a few spots down the table. "I should have her out to the ranch."

"You should, Mom," Harvey said, looking from her back to Flynn. "You're a good man, Flynn. Keeping Widow Jones's property up to snuff."

"Thank you, sir," Flynn said, but he didn't feel like a good man. Would a good man go out with his boss's daughter behind the boss's back?

Somehow, he didn't think so.

Besides, he helped Widow Jones with basic things. Lawn care in the summer and snow removal in the winter. He checked on her almost every day, and brought her groceries in between her weekly deliveries if she needed them.

He did visit his mother as much as possible, as his only sibling lived an hour north of Lewiston. And Wendy was married, with two kids. She couldn't get down as often as she'd like.

"I saw your dad's old place go up for sale this week," Harvey said, and Flynn dropped his piece of pizza.

"What?" he asked.

"Your place went up for sale," he said again. "I guess the Washburns are going back to Virginia. The price is high, but I heard they've done a ton of improvements on the house, the land, the outbuildings. All of it." He took another bite of pizza as if he hadn't just blown Flynn's whole world wide open.

Jessie sat down next to him, a completely normal thing to do, as Betsy filled in the spot beside her. "You should go look at the place," she said. "Maybe you could buy it back."

Flynn just looked at her, unsure of what to say. He'd never told anyone how deep the wound was over losing the farm. "Maybe," he said, knowing he couldn't afford the farm. Sure, he had a little bit of money, but he wasn't wealthy by any means.

The conversation moved to something else, and most of the attention moved down the table to the Locke brothers, who were telling a story from their childhood.

Jessie twisted toward him slightly and whispered, "I'll go with you, if you want."

He nodded, because he'd like that very much. He'd get to see her and spend time with her, and no one could call walking through memories a date.

THE NEXT MORNING, FLYNN GOT TO WORK ON THE widow's yard early, before the sun could heat the earth beyond bearable. It wasn't quite July yet, but Idaho had a funny way about the weather. Some days would be scorching, and by afternoon, the rainclouds would roll in.

Flynn didn't check the weather, unless opening the door and deciding if he needed a jacket or not counted. He knew it was bright and warm that morning, and he got the lawn mowed before heading back to his tiny house next door to Widow Jones. He'd just finished mowing his own lawn when his phone rang.

Jenny Pedraco.

"Flynn," she said when he'd answered. "I got your message, and we can go look at that farm any time you want. The family has already vacated the premises."

"They have?"

"Yes, they had to move suddenly, and apparently, the wife just returned this week to finish getting it ready to list."

"Great," he said, thinking about Jess and when she might be able to go. "When are you free?"

"How about this afternoon?" she asked. "I have an open house until one, and then I can go. Say, three or so?"

"That should work," he said. "I'll text you for sure in a minute. I need to check with someone."

"Sounds good." Jenny hung up, and Flynn appreciated her no-nonsense approach to real estate. She'd sold the farm all those years ago, and she'd helped Flynn find his place in town too.

He dialed Jess, hoping she was somewhere where she could talk. He knew Rhodes worked the ranch on weekends, and sometimes Flynn did too. It happened to be his weekend off, and he'd like to fill it with all things Jess if he could.

"Hey there," she said, her voice already filled with flirt. He wondered why she seemed upset with him over the flirting he did with other women when she was seriously the biggest flirt he knew.

"Hey," he said. "I can go see the farm this afternoon at three. Are you still in?"

"Of course," she said.

"You can get away from the ranch?"

"I'm already done with the essential chores."

"Good," he said, pushing his hat back and wiping his hand through his hair. "Maybe you'd like to come eat lunch with me."

A beat of silence passed, and a flash of frustration filled

Flynn at the same time. He'd thought they were past this. She'd agreed to keep things below board for now; she'd called him her boyfriend.

"I'd like that," she said. "When?"

"Whenever you want," he said. "I'll text you my address." She couldn't get there faster than he could shower, even if she left as soon as they hung up. Which she wouldn't. Flynn had the feeling Jess knew exactly how to be in a relationship, though she'd been in very few that he knew of.

"All right," she said. "I have to stop by my granny's, and then I'll head into town."

JESS DIDN'T ARRIVE FOR ANOTHER HOUR AND A HALF. Flynn didn't care, as it was actually lunch time when she pulled up in that old blue and white truck she rumbled around the ranch in. He watched her through the window, and she checked her appearance in the rear-view mirror and seemed to be talking to herself.

He wasn't sure what that was about, but he stepped away from the window and went out onto the front porch. She saw him and got out of the truck. "Nice place," she said, taking in the house in one sweeping glance.

"It's small," he said. "But it does just fine." His dogs got up when Jess came up the steps, their noses already sniffing. "Leave her be," he told them.

But Jess didn't leave them alone. She crouched down right in front of Shep and started stroking her hands down both sides of his face. "Oh, hey, you old man," she said. "What's he? Like, eight now?"

"Nine," Flynn said. "Sally's eight."

"That's right." Jess let Sally lick her face, and Flynn shook his head.

"Gross," he said. "I can't believe you let her do that."

"She likes it, don't you?" She grinned at the dog and finally stood up. Flynn wanted to kiss her cheek too, but he didn't need dog slobber on his mouth, thank you very much.

"Come on in," he said. "I'll give you the grand tour. This is the porch." He gestured to it. He had a rocking chair out here he rarely used. "The dogs like it here." He stepped inside, where a small living room bled back into the kitchen area. A set of steps went up just inside the front door, and he had two bedrooms and a bathroom up there.

"Bedrooms upstairs," he said, deciding not to do the *grand* tour. "Living room. Kitchen. Bathroom behind the steps. Laundry room. Back door."

Jess looked around at everything, picked up a picture of him and his parents on graduation day, smiled at it, and set it back down. "Are we ordering lunch? Or...?"

"No, I'll cook," he said. "I mean, cook is such a relative term, don't you think?" He got out a pan and put it on the stove. "Are you okay with grilled ham and cheese sandwiches?"

"I'm okay with whatever," she said. "I'm not a great cook."

"Neither am I," he said. "I can do a few things. Nothing big." He got to work buttering bread and slicing cheese. "What did Granny want this morning?"

"Oh, she lectured me about finding a husband now that I'm thirty."

"You're kidding."

"I wish." Jess sat at the bar and watched him work. "You don't think thirty is too old, do you?"

"Not at all," he said. "I mean, look at Betsy. She's what? Thirty-something." He actually only kept track of Jess's important dates, and that fact didn't escape him. "And she and Knox aren't even engaged yet."

"They will be," Jess said quietly. "And she's thirty-four."

"There you go. Has Granny been lecturing her?"

"I don't think my grandmother knows what to do with a woman like me," Jess said. "Honestly, I don't. It's nothing against her. She just doesn't...get me."

Flynn looked at Jessie and found the worry and sadness on her face. "Well, not everyone can be the same."

She didn't say anything, and Flynn got the sandwiches into the pan before turning back to her. "Jess, you're a great woman. Strong, hardworking. You know more about horses and cattle than anyone I've ever met. You're gorgeous, and, I don't know." He shrugged. "If your grandmother can't see any of that, then that's her loss."

"It's all of those things you just said that she doesn't get."

"So what?" he asked. "You're going to let it define you?"

"No," she said, the softness in her eyes turning hard.

"Good," he said, pulling a spatula from the drawer so he could flip the sandwiches. "You said you know who I am, and Jess, trust me when I say I have a pretty good idea of who you are too. And you're amazing."

A smile bloomed on her face, and Flynn was glad he could put it there. It was nice being real with someone, and he flipped their sandwiches before saying, "I've never had a woman over to my house before."

"I don't believe that," she said. "You've been out with *so many* women."

He cringed, but he didn't argue with her. "You don't go out much."

"No one asks me," she said. "They see Cami, or they see Georgia. Never me."

"I see you," he said, turning around to get plates out of the cupboard.

"I know," she said. "It's kind of weird."

"Why?" He slid a sandwich onto one plate, and then the next.

"I don't know," she said. "You're like, this amazing man, and I'm just Jessie."

Flynn gaped at her. "You have no idea how backward that sentence is." She looked at him, and Flynn grinned. He moved around to the bar and sat beside her. "Hold my hand while I say grace."

"You just want to hold my hand," she teased.

"Yep," he said, still waiting for her to put her hand in his. "Come on, now. I won't bite."

Jess finally slipped her hand into his, and he laced their fingers together nice and tight. She made him feel more whole than he had in five long years, and he bent his head, a silent prayer of gratitude lifting up to God before he said grace over their lunch.

Flynn knew how to get women. He simply didn't know how to keep them. So after he said, "Amen," and she echoed it, he added silently, *Please help me with this one, Lord. I don't want to hurt her, and I don't want to lose her.*

As they started eating, Flynn had the distinct thought that he'd have to *be truthful* with her. And that tied his stomach in knots.

CHAPTER FIVE

"Flynn, this place is *nice*." Jessie couldn't seem to take everything in at once, and she stood just underneath the arch announcing their arrival at Twin Sisters Ranch.

"The name would need to change," he said.

"That's easy," she said, slipping her hand into his. Tension radiated from his broad shoulders in waves, and she wanted him to go back to his easy, casual, laid-back self. But Jessie was beginning to realize that was the façade Flynn put on for everyone else to see.

And she got to see the man who worried after his neighbors and knew how to make perfectly crispy, melty grilled sandwiches, and who desperately wanted his father's farm back.

"What happened?" she asked.

"Dad didn't have a will," he said, his voice hollow. "No estate planning. Nothing legal. So things fell to my mother, and we didn't have family trying to take things from us or anything." He started walking, though the real estate agent hadn't arrived yet.

The barns and cabins Jessie could see from here looked pristine, with fresh coats of paint. She couldn't wait to get inside and see what they looked like. The homestead sat down the lane a ways, and Flynn couldn't seem to look away from it.

Along the sides of the road, the fields of grass and hay waved in the breeze, and she wanted Flynn to get this place back.

This was where he belonged, not on her family's ranch. Not working land for someone else.

"Dad had a piece of paper that said Wendy and I got a small sum of money, and my mother honored that, though it wasn't legal, and she didn't have to give it to us. Then we found out my dad had been terrible at finances. The farm was in debt, and the only way my mother could get out was to sell the place." He stopped walking, his throat working against itself as he swallowed. "So she sold the place and moved to Lewiston. She got enough to pay off the debts and buy her condo."

Jessie's heart tore for this cowboy. "All these years," she said. "You never told me."

"Nothing to tell." He cleared his throat. "I've been happy at Quinn Valley."

Jessie shook her head, but she decided not to argue. If Flynn had truly been happy, he wouldn't have tried to fill his life with dancing and women for the past five years. No, the loss of this ranch had cut him deeply, and those things were Band-Aids when he needed surgery.

She kept all of that to herself, wondering if there was more about him that she didn't know.

Of course there is, she told herself. But she didn't need to learn it all today.

The sound of a car pulling up came from behind her, and Jessie turned, a prayer in her heart that the Lord would help

Flynn get this ranch back.

"There's Jenny," he said as the severe blonde woman got out of her sports car. She wore a crisp gray pantsuit that looked like it belonged in a board room and not on a ranch.

Flynn smiled at her and shook her hand, introducing Jessie as "a friend of mine."

Jessie cringed inwardly at the label, but she couldn't have him broadcasting their relationship, even to a real estate agent who probably didn't know a single Quinn. Still, the degrees of separation in Quinn Valley weren't nearly as large as the six for other people around the world.

"Let's start with the land," she said. "Forrest Washburn acquired seventeen more deeds to water rights three years ago. That's more than enough for the acreage of this place, which is—"

"Nine hundred acres," Flynn said. "I know."

"It's planted already," Jenny continued as if she hadn't heard the hollow quality of Flynn's voice. But Jessie heard it. "It comes with all the animals, and a neighbor is taking care of them until the ranch sells. The Washburns had a family emergency in Virginia, and they decided suddenly to move."

"Can we look around?" Flynn asked.

"Of course," Jenny said. "Would you like to start in the homestead? It's been completely redone, Flynn. It would be a fresh start for you here."

He nodded, his hand gripping Jessie's too tightly. She pulled away, and he said, "Sorry. I guess I'm a little nervous." They walked back to his truck, and Jessie climbed in, still trying to find the right words to say.

"Maybe you should pray about it," she said quietly. He sat behind the wheel, the air conditioner blowing, as the red sports car kicked up dust as Jenny drove down the lane toward the homestead.

"Would you?" Flynn asked, looking at Jessie. In that

moment, Jessie felt herself slipping further in love with him, as if she wasn't in deep enough already.

"Sure," she said, her voice a bit froggy. As she prayed that Flynn would have the clarity of mind about the ranch, and that he would know what God wanted him to do, and that she could support him any way possible, she felt sure she'd revealed too many of her feelings.

When she finished, Flynn reached for her. She slid across the seat and let him hold her. "Thank you, sweetheart," he whispered into her hair, and Jessie felt more content than she had in years.

JESSIE MADE IT THROUGH CHURCH THE NEXT DAY WITHOUT revealing her new relationship. Flynn didn't come to lunch, and he sat way down on the end of the row beside her father, as usual. Well, sometimes he sat by Rhodes or Logan or whoever. Sometimes her, and she'd never suspected that he liked her for more than one of the ranch hands.

He was exceptionally good at hiding things, and that kept Jessie awake at night when she wished it wouldn't.

Her work around the ranch didn't feel like drudgery anymore. When she heard Flynn whistling, her heart catapulted around inside her chest, and when he came to see her in the morning in the calf barn, she experienced more joy than she knew how to contain.

"Come to my place tonight," he whispered a week after her birthday party, his lips right at her ear. He hadn't kissed her yet, but the soft, secret touches were thrilling enough. He held her now, swaying with his eyes closed as they breathed together.

"What did you decide about the ranch?" she asked.

"I'm working with the bank," he said. "I think I'm going to get approved. They said I'd know by Monday."

"What are we going to do at your place tonight?" She smiled up at him, the idea of kissing him all she could think about.

"I don't know," he said. "It's been a rough week. Maybe we'll just hide out and watch a movie. I know how to make churro popcorn."

"You won't be missed at the dancehall?"

His eyes flew open, and Jessie hated that she'd brought up his dancing habit. "Jess." He dropped his arms from around her, and she felt cold though July was right around the corner.

"Sorry," she said quickly. "It's just...maybe I don't want to hide out with you inside your house."

"Oh, you want everyone to know about us." His eyes sparkled as he teased her, but Jessie felt stupid.

"Kind of," she said, though there was no kind of about it. Other women got to parade Flynn around on their arms, and she'd always wondered what that would be like. How everyone would look at her and wonder how she'd gotten him to go out with her.

Her.

Everyone would see her then. Everyone would know her name; she wouldn't just be "one of the Quinns" or "Rhodes's little sister," or "the one older than Cami."

"Well, that's up to you, sweetheart," he said. "I told you I didn't care if your dad or Rhodes knew. You seemed like you wanted to keep things under wraps for a while."

"I did," she said, now wondering why.

"Why's that?" he asked.

"I...wasn't sure you weren't just being nice to me." She lifted her chin, almost daring him to confirm what she'd said.

A pinch of pain entered his eyes, and he opened his

mouth to say something at the same time the barn door squeaked as someone came in.

He jumped away from her, swiping his hat off his head and putting it back on, all in the space of a breath. "So I'll see you over in the hay barn," he said. "Bring that clipboard, would you? I'll give it to Clay."

His voice sounded so unlike the boyfriend Flynn Jessie had been talking to, and he walked away without waiting for her to say anything. "Oh, good morning, Clay," he said, and Jessie turned from her workbench to find the other cowboy moving the ladder so he could climb into the loft, where they stored a few things. "He's here, Jess. You can just give it to him."

"Morning, Jess," Clay said as if he hadn't interrupted anything. And of course, he didn't know he had.

"Hey," she said, glad her voice sounded normal, as Flynn slipped out of the barn. "Everything okay out there?" He didn't normally come and get the medication charts from her, but they met over near the small office he maintained in the stables. As the veterinarian for the ranch, Clay lived on-site and worked seven days a week.

"Yep," he said. "Rhodes just wants the tent down. Getting ready for the Fourth."

"Oh, right. The charts are almost done."

"Great." Clay climbed up into the loft and tossed down a few boxes, all of them making extremely loud noises as they landed. "Sorry," he said, climbing down.

"It's fine," she said, going over to help him. "Where does he want these?"

"I have the ATV with the trailer," Clay said. "I'll take them out to the field just east of the homestead." He gave her a smile and paused. "Hey, can I ask you a question?"

"Sure." Jessie bent to pick up one of the lighter boxes anyway.

"Is Cami...I mean.... Oh, wow. Forget it." His face turned bright red, and he ducked out of the barn as quickly as he'd come.

Jessie grinned and followed him. "She just broke up with this loser boyfriend of hers," she said without looking at Clay. "Maybe give her a few weeks, and then be *really* nice to her." She turned around to go back inside the barn to finish her medication charts for the day. "I'll have your charts in five minutes, if you want to wait."

"Sure." He continued taking boxes out while Jessie finished up the charts.

Outside, she smiled and handed them to him with the words, "Really nice, Clay. Cami's had a string of not-nice men in her life."

He nodded, pressed his lips together, and studied something on the horizon. "How many weeks should I wait?"

"Maybe let her know you're interested now," Jessie said. "But don't ask her out for a couple of weeks."

He nodded, got in the ATV, and revved away.

Jessie turned toward the hay barn in the distance, thinking it needed new paint now that she'd seen the facilities at Flynn's ranch.

Almost his ranch.

Her phone went off as she walked between the barns, and a text from Cami sat on her screen. *Just got asked out by Malcolm! I should say yes, right?*

Jessie's heart fell to her boot tips. *If you want to*, she texted back.

I do, Cami said. *He's so dreamy.*

Malcolm had just been hired on at the ranch, and Jessie found him to be too old for her, let alone her younger sister. But Cami had a magnetism about her that attracted everyone, and it was no wonder Clay wanted to ask her out.

Her pulse didn't accelerate with lost hope the way it

usually did. She was seeing Flynn, though no one knew it. She'd always been happy for Cami in her relationships, but she didn't want to be the last Quinn sibling without a date to all the family functions.

"Just hire someone," she muttered to herself as she thought about Georgia and Logan. "That worked."

But she knew it wouldn't work for her. She pushed into the barn to hear Rhodes talking with Flynn.

"So you're telling me you haven't been out with anyone?" her brother asked. "You know I can find out."

"I've stayed away from the dancehall," Flynn said. "No females in my life, just like I said."

Jess's breath left her body in one fell swoop. *No females in my life.* What did that mean? Part of her wanted to run. Find a spot behind a barn and cry.

The other part demanded to know what Flynn meant by that, consequences or not. "Hey," she said, marching around the corner and into the tack room, where they stood talking. "No females? You?"

Rhodes started laughing. "Even Jess doesn't believe you." He grinned at her. "He made a deal with me and Newt. No dates, no new girls, for thirty days, or he has to buy us all a nice steak dinner. His time's almost up."

Jessie looked at Flynn, her eyebrows sky high. "It is, is it?"

"Jess," he said, his smile stuck in place, but his eyes filled with absolute terror.

Good, Jessie thought. *Let him squirm.*

She scoffed and said, "I'm going out to the pasture with Wyatt. He's not on a *female fast,* is he?"

"What?" Rhodes asked, but Jessie just turned and walked away, the sound of Flynn's sigh filling the space between her footsteps.

CHAPTER SIX

Flynn escaped the hay barn without telling Rhodes anything. He knew Rhodes and Jessie were close, and he didn't have the stomach to tell his best friend he'd been holding his sister's hand. Not until the female fast ended, and not until Jess gave him the go-ahead.

And now, she likely wouldn't. He couldn't even get her to answer his texts. He read through them again, and they sounded desperate even to him.

In the end, he made one more desperate move. He texted Wyatt. *Is Jess with you?*

Right here, he said.

Can you ask her to call me?

Several seconds passed, and then Wyatt's message said, *She just laughed and said right. I don't get it.*

"Never mind," Flynn muttered to himself as he stuffed his phone in his back pocket. She had a stubborn streak he normally admired—when it wasn't aimed at him. He knew where she was, and he could go talk to her if he wanted to. Instead, he opted to let her cool off a little, absorb his texts.

You're obviously not the normal female I'd be going out with, he'd said. *The fast didn't apply to you.*

He wasn't sure if that made him more of a player or not. He didn't want to fool around with Jess and break her heart. She'd been there for him last weekend when he'd needed her, just like she had been since the moment he'd arrived at Quinn Valley Ranch. She was kind, beautiful, and everything he'd always wanted.

"You're going to have to tell her about Sandra," he muttered to himself as he put on a pair of gloves and headed out to the equipment shed. He'd get the hay mowed in the fields he'd been assigned, and then he'd find Jess.

She still hadn't answered him about coming to his house that night, and he didn't want to be alone.

He didn't know *how* to be alone. Everyone and everything had abandoned him so quickly, his life had been full of holes. He'd needed something or someone to fill them, and ranch work and best friends only went so far.

In the past week, as he spent more time with Jess hiding in the barn, or texting her at night, those holes didn't exist.

Behind the wheel of the tractor, he pulled off his gloves and sent her another message. *Listen, maybe I messed up. I don't know. I'm sorry. Please come to dinner at my place tonight.*

I want a steak dinner too. The message that popped up actually made him smile.

Deal. He just wanted her to come.

I'm still really annoyed with you, just to be clear.

Why? he texted. *I broke my deal with my friends to see you. Isn't that a compliment?*

No, Flynn, it means you'll flirt with the first girl who shows any interest in you at all. I'm not interested in being that girl. If that's what we are...I don't want that to be what we are.

"Jess," he said aloud, only his ears close enough to hear the anguish in his voice. "That's not what you are."

Be truthful.

The words from the Lord were still there, and Flynn's fingers flew across the screen. *I have to tell you something about my last real girlfriend. Will you please come tonight? Steak and seafood, if that's what you want. Just come.*

He deleted off the last two words, so he didn't come across too dramatic. Satisfied with the message, he sent it.

Fine.

Relief hit him with her response, even though he knew that was the worst word a female could use. Now, he better get his chores done so he could get off this ranch, order dinner, shower, and be ready to talk to Jess when she showed up.

FLYNN SAT IN THE CHAIR ON HIS FRONT PORCH, BOTH OF his dogs panting at his feet. He'd thrown a ball for them for thirty minutes, received the dinners he'd ordered ten minutes ago, and Jess still wasn't here.

He found a single word moving through his mind—*please*—his right foot tapping out a rhythm on the floorboards at his feet.

Jess finally pulled up in that white ranch truck, jumping down and closing the door behind her. She adjusted the tie on the bottom of her blouse and inhaled deeply, her chest lifting, before Flynn stood up.

She stalled, and he came down the steps to meet her. "Heya, Jess."

"Oh, you don't get to talk to me in that sweet voice," she said. "I'm going to be mad all the way through dinner."

He shook his head as he smiled. "All right. It's inside. Let's get it over with, so you'll forgive me."

She stepped ahead of him, and Flynn didn't feel bad about

watching her climb the steps ahead of him. She paused to pet his pups, and he watched Shep close his eyes in bliss. Flynn knew how he felt, and he busied himself inside by getting down real dishes and serving up the food.

"Medium-rare," he said. "Which you didn't even tell me. I just know that's what you like."

She glanced up at him and rolled her eyes. "It's not hard," she said. "You've eaten with my family a million times."

"I don't know what Cami likes."

"I don't believe you."

"Ask me," he said, sitting down across from her, determined to show her he'd liked her for a long time.

"I don't know what to ask," she said, cutting into her baked potato.

"Okay, I'll talk," he said. "One time, all of you girls went to get your hair done. It was for your parents' thirty-fifth wedding anniversary. You got your hair colored, and it was this beautiful, silky shade of blonde I wanted to run my fingers through." He cut a bite of steak and put it in his mouth, watching her.

She'd stilled, and she finally lifted her eyes to his. "What color was Betsy's hair?"

"I have no idea. I only saw you." He put down his knife and fork. "Jess, I saw you when you cried on the north side of the stables after that jerk Winn broke up with you three years ago. I saw you when you held onto that rope, even when the cow on the other end of it could've ripped your shoulders right out of their sockets."

He swallowed, but he was just getting started, and he'd never fought this hard to keep a woman in his life before. He didn't know what it meant, but he didn't want to stop, didn't want to lose her. "I saw you when you showed up at the dancehall a few months ago. You looked around, and I thought I was finally going to get to hold you in my arms. Then you took one look at me and walked out."

His heart felt too big for his chest. "I'm sorry, sweetheart. I didn't mean to hurt you. The female fast is stupid. Even Rhodes knew I wouldn't really do it. But the point is, I didn't break it for someone I don't care about." He reached across the table and covered her hand with his, encouraged when she didn't pull away.

"What did you have to tell me about your last real girlfriend?"

Flynn sat back in his chair, folding his hands in his lap. "Her name was Sandra Iverson. You know the Iverson's, I assume."

"Yes," she said. "Sandra left town a few...years ago."

"Five years ago," Flynn said, his throat narrowing. Why hadn't he eaten first too? This conversation would probably be easier if he had. "Two weeks before my father died, in fact. I was heartbroken. I was in love with her, and we'd been together for three years. I bought her a diamond ring and asked her to marry me. As she stood above me, crying, she said she didn't want to be a rancher's wife."

Flynn shook his head. "I didn't see it. I didn't see her. I didn't know. I was so...stupid." The memories wouldn't go away now that he'd let them out of their box. "She left town the next day. Then my dad died. I lost him at a crucial time in my life, and I was angry with everyone. Him, for dying. My mom, for not knowing the state of the ranch. Myself, for being as clueless as she was. Sandra, for abandoning me. God, for everything."

He looked up, the familiar bitterness and hopelessness coursing through him again. "Then I lost the ranch too. Just like that. One, two, three things I loved gone. I felt so alone."

Jessie wiped her eyes, but she said nothing.

"I called Rhodes, and that man saved me." He leaned forward, hoping he could keep his own emotions dormant long enough to be truthful, the way he felt like he needed to be.

"Your dad saved me. Your mom. The ranch. And you, Jess. You were so kind to me, and you taught me how to treat others as if they'd just lost their girlfriend, their father, and their ranch in the span of three weeks."

He swallowed. "I was sick for a long time, but you were always there, always with a smile or a helping hand."

"Stop it," she said, sniffling. "Just stop it. I didn't do anything special."

But she had, and he'd never told anyone any of this. "I started having romantic feelings for you when I found a way to move past Sandra."

"How long?" she asked.

"Years," he whispered. "I've thought about kissing you for years, Jess."

She stared at him, her eyes glassy. A tear fell down her cheek, and she swiped at it as she exploded out of her chair. "Excuse me."

"Jess," he said after her, but she strode out of the front door without looking back, those reddish-blonde curls begging him to touch them. "You've done it now, cowboy," he said to himself, something his father used to say to the men who worked the ranch with them.

He got up and went to the front door too, only to find Jess had left in her blue and white truck. Helplessness filled him, and he turned to his two cattle dogs. "I blew it with her, didn't I?"

Sally got up and stretched, making a yowling sound as she yawned too. He wasn't sure what she was trying to say, because Flynn didn't understand dog language.

But he knew Jess, and he hurried back into the house and grabbed his keys.

He knew right where she'd go, and he wasn't going to let her abandon him the way everyone else had.

CHAPTER SEVEN

——————

"Wow," Ivy said as she slid into the booth across from Jessie. "You've already eaten half of this."

"Yeah," Jessie said, glancing up at her cousin. She should've known better than to come to the pub, but it was her go-to place to regroup. Find her center. Fill up with chocolate and ice cream, which somehow made her mind work better.

At least that was what she told herself.

"Problems at the ranch?" Ivy glanced toward the kitchen, where she'd probably need to get back to work.

Jessie shook her head, though she didn't want to talk about Flynn either. It simply irked her that her own cousin assumed her bad mood came from the ranch. As if cows held the power to make her have a good day or a bad one.

No, that power seemed to belong to Flynn and no one else. She almost scoffed. How could he have been thinking about kissing her for years?

He was either a liar or a magician at hiding how he felt.

"We should go to lunch," Ivy said. "I think you might have something to tell me."

"Do I?" Jessie asked.

"Oh, definitely." Ivy slid out of the booth and stepped closer to Jessie. "Something named Flynn Hollister, who's coming this way now."

Jessie's heart bumped irregularly, and she scooped up another bite of baked brownie bliss as if she didn't care who was coming her way.

"Yeah, like you have something to tell me about Nash," Jessie said.

Ivy only giggled and walked away, and Jessie really would have to go to lunch with her later and fill her in. Ivy would text relentlessly until she did. But at least she'd get some gossip about her cousin's love life too. She'd seen the country music star around town, and Ivy was a star with a guitar, just waiting to be born.

When Flynn sat down across from her, she put the treat in her mouth and looked at him. She couldn't believe he'd liked her for so long and done nothing about it.

"You should've told me," she said, licking her spoon clean and handing it to him.

He took it and focused on the ice cream and brownie between them. "Why does it matter?"

"I was going to leave the ranch," she said. "Because of you. Because I couldn't stand to be so close to you and not be yours."

He lifted his eyes to hers, and she drowned in the dark depths of them. "You're mine," he said. "If you want to be."

She nodded, happiness driving out some of the despair that had filled her. "I felt like I was being so obvious these last few months."

"Maybe you were," he said. "I don't know. I had to put my

fantasies about us out of my mind, or I would've gone crazy at the ranch too."

"Did you like any of those other women you went out with?"

"You don't need to torture yourself about them," he said.

"*You* tortured me with them," she pointed out.

"They were all a poor substitute for you," he said. "But I was convinced I couldn't have you. Number one, I'm a lot older than you."

"Six years isn't that much older."

"And yet, I heard Cami's going out with Malcolm and everyone's saying how he's too old for her." Flynn cocked his head. "You realize they're six years apart, right?"

"Do we need another spoon here?"

Jessie glanced up at the waitress. "Yes, please. He stole mine."

"Be right back."

Flynn handed her spoon back to her, and she simply looked from it to him. "I'm sorry," he said. "For everything. I just—I don't care about a female fast, and I don't care about anyone I've been out with or danced with or kissed in the past five years. Just you, Jess."

Warmth filled her from sole to skull, and she nodded. "All right."

He glanced around the pub where she'd escaped. "And we're out now, sweetheart. In public."

"I suppose so."

"So I'll save you a seat by me at church tomorrow."

Jessie's eyebrows went up. "You think so?"

"I told you, I don't have a problem with dating you."

"Maybe you should let your female fast run out. See if you can trick Rhodes and Newt into believing you did it." She leaned forward, feeling flirty and dangerous now. "And we need to make it through the Fourth of July with all my cousins and aunts and uncles."

"So a few more days," he said. "Then we can go dancing next weekend."

She shook her head. "Flynn, I'm not a dancer."

"I'll teach you," he said, and the thought of him showing her how to move, where to put her hands, and holding her close had her heart twittering in her chest.

"Would you guys like more than dessert?" the waitress asked as she set another spoon on the table in front of Flynn.

"No," he said, pulling out his wallet. "Just this, thanks."

She smiled at him, took his card, and walked away.

"Our steaks will be cold," Jessie said.

"Then I'll put in a pizza," he said. "I just...I'm not in the mood to be out. I just want to be at home with you."

She liked the sound of that, and she hurried to finish the cast iron skillet full of brownie and ice cream so she could go back to Flynn's house and lay in the comfort and security of his arms.

JESSIE ENDURED CHURCH THE NEXT DAY, HAVING TOLD Rhodes about Malcolm asking Cami on a date. Her brother hadn't been happy about that, and she couldn't enjoy the sermon for all her wondering about what he'd say about her and Flynn.

He'd claimed Malcolm was "much too old" for Cami, but Flynn's words about how he and she were the same age difference kept her from focusing on anything else.

She had a few chores after church and dinner with her family, and she took her time out on the ranch. The land radiated peace to her, a sense of serenity she couldn't find anywhere else. Not that she'd really tried.

She'd been born and raised in Quinn Valley and had no desire to leave town—at least now that Flynn had confessed his feelings for her.

The landscaping at the homestead was coming along nicely, and it felt like the ranch was holding its breath for the next big thing to happen. Everyone in the Quinn family would be coming out for the Fourth of July celebration, and Jessie normally liked having all of her aunts and uncles, cousins and significant others, around.

But this year, she felt...off.

"What is it, Lord?" she asked, finally feeling that calmness she usually found at church. God didn't answer her, but then again, He'd never spoken in a loud voice, with thunder and the shaking of the Earth.

Jessie still felt Him nearby, carefully watching over her and her family. "And Flynn," she murmured. He'd said he'd been mad at God, but he'd gone to church every week since she'd known him. He couldn't have been that mad.

Or maybe he viewed church the way Jessie did—as a sanctuary. A hospital for the sick and weary, for those simply doing their best and trying their hardest.

"Please help Flynn get his ranch back," she said to the puffy, white clouds as they moved through the sky. "Help him find happiness."

She could see now how many fronts the man had up, though he claimed to really love dancing. "Might as well have some fun, right?" he'd said last night after they'd gone back to his house to finish their steak dinners. "None of those women meant anything to me, Jess."

She believed him, and she hoped with everything in her that she wouldn't be left feeling foolish because of it.

The days passed, with Flynn stopping by in the morning to have a private hello with her. He hadn't kissed her yet, and Jessie honestly wondered if he would. He seemed...careful with her in a way he didn't exhibit around others, but he didn't have a problem holding her hand, or touching her hair, or holding her close to his heart.

The morning of the Fourth dawned bright and early, and Jessie got out of bed with the sun so she could get the bulk of her chores done before the family picnic—and the heat.

Betsy was already up and cooking in the kitchen, their mother helping as Jessie and Cami pulled on their cowgirl boots. As Jessie waited for her toast to pop up, the front door opened and Granny walked in with Rhodes and his new girlfriend, who was also the landscaper, Capri Harwood.

He didn't have to worry about older brothers or younger sisters approving of his boyfriend, though Jessie knew he worried about plenty of other things. "Morning, dear," Granny said, smiling at Jessie. She wore a perfectly pressed pair of navy blue slacks with a red, white, and blue blouse.

"You're so festive," Jessie said, hugging her grandmother. She always was. The woman had rings and earrings for every holiday, and she never let an opportunity go by without dressing to the nines and looking her best.

"I love the Fourth of July," she said. "And toast."

Jessie giggled as she buttered her toast and handed it to Granny. "There you go, Granny."

"Oh, I can't take your toast." But she bit into the buttery, crispy slice of bread as Jessie put down two more pieces. "Did you impress someone at that card game?"

Jessie's first reaction was to sigh and say no. Instead, she tilted her head and looked at Granny. "Maybe."

Granny grinned, her bright blue eyes sparkling like sapphires. "I knew there would be someone there for you."

"But it's all the same men," Jessie said. "How did you know?"

"When you get to be my age, dear, you can smell things in the air." She laughed, her voice a little scratchy, telling the world how much wisdom she had from the years she'd spent on this planet.

"You must really be smelling a lot, then," Jessie said, reaching for the toast as it popped up. "Rhodes has a new girlfriend. Robyn and Ben—I know that marriage contract had your name written all over it. Riley just got engaged too." Jessie lifted her eyebrows, almost daring Granny to argue with her.

"It's a curse," Granny said with another laugh.

"I'll bet," Jessie said dryly, taking her toast with her toward the mudroom. She stuffed her hat on her head with one hand while she held a piece of toast in her mouth.

She couldn't help scanning the ranch beyond the house where her parents lived, because she often saw Flynn at work out in the fields in the morning.

Today, though, Rhodes had a dozen men out in the field just south of the homestead, erecting the huge tents that would shade the family later that day.

"I'm not going to go out with Malcolm," Cami said, stepping to Jessie's side and startling her.

"Where did you come from?"

"I was waiting for you to come out," Cami said with a smile.

"So no Malcolm? Why?"

Cami shrugged, though there had to be a reason. Jessie didn't like it when her sisters pressured her to say more, so she didn't ask again. Cami wasn't usually reserved, and she and Jessie were close.

"Remember how I told you about that cowboy I liked?" Jessie asked.

"Yes," Cami said slowly, her eyes glued to the side of Jessie's face now.

"He asked me out."

Cami's face split into a grin. "That's great, Jess. Is that where you've been disappearing to at night?"

"A couple of times," she said. "It's not like I go see…him all the time."

"You were gone almost all day and all night on Saturday."

"I was helping Granny all morning," she said. "I didn't even go to town until afternoon."

"And the Saturday before that."

"That was—yeah," she said.

"So," Cami said. "Who is it?"

"I'm not sure I'm ready to tell," Jessie said. Flynn had said he didn't care who knew, and Jessie realized it was all her holding them in the shadows.

"He works here, doesn't he?" Cami stopped and looked toward the group putting up the tent. "Is he over there?"

Flynn indeed stood at one of the corners, holding the ropes with two gloved hands. "Yes," Jessie said.

"Oh, girl, you sighed that." Cami burst out laughing. "Yes." She exaggerated the breathiness of the word and dragged it out way too long.

Jessie could only smile, because she'd heard the soft emotions in her voice. "If I tell you, will you promise not to tell anyone? I want to talk to Rhodes about it first."

"That's a good idea," Cami said. "He wasn't happy about Malcolm asking me out."

Jessie watched Wyatt point to something and Clay reach for another section of the tent. Jessie understood Rhodes better than her other sisters did, but she didn't tell Cami that.

"It's Flynn," she said, turning her back on him and heading toward the calf barn where she started all of her mornings, holiday or not.

"Flynn?" The level of shock in Cami's voice could not have been louder. "Are you kidding?"

"No," Jessie said, not slowing as Cami darted in front of her.

"Jess." Cami touched her arm to get her to stop, and Jessie sighed as she did. Telling her sister had been a mistake, and it had only been ten seconds.

"He dates everyone," Cami said.

"I know," Jessie said.

"He's not serious about anyone."

She thought of all the very serious conversations they'd had in the past couple of weeks. "I know."

"How long have you liked him?"

"A long time."

"And he asked you out? When?"

"Poker night a couple of weeks ago." Jessie sighed and adjusted her hat. "Can we not discuss it to death? We're getting to know each other better, that's all." She stepped around her sister, knowing full well she was doing more than that.

She was praying for him, and helping him with his ranch, and dreaming of a future with him.

"Okay, okay," Cami said. "But wow. Flynn Hollister, going out with someone for a couple of weeks. That's a record or something, right?"

Irritation ate through Jessie, and she gritted her teeth so she wouldn't say something rude to Cami. "Don't tell anyone," she said when they reached the calf barn.

"My lips are sealed," Cami said, continuing over to the chicken coops, where her day usually began.

"Please help Cami keep her mouth shut," Jessie muttered, and then she determined she wasn't going to pray for every little thing that day.

CHAPTER EIGHT

Flynn liked his new morning routine. He let the dogs out of the back of his truck, and they went tearing off into the cattle pastures. He worked in the fields near the homestead, checking fences and chutes as sometimes the "troublemaker" cows in this pasture chewed through things in the night. He fed and watered them, then moved to the stables.

He slipped away each morning when he knew Rhodes would be busy with something else. Now that his best friend was dating Capri, Rhodes didn't have his eye on every little thing around the ranch, freeing Flynn up to spend more time with Jessie in the calf barn.

Hardly anyone came in there, and she'd started bringing him toaster pastries and those little cartons of chocolate milk he'd enjoyed growing up in elementary school.

They'd been getting along really well, and Flynn pushed into the barn a few days after the Fourth of July to find her bent over her workbench, her hair falling over her shoulders in a soft, sexy way.

"Morning, sweetheart," he said, taking her into his arms.

"Hey." She wore a smile in her voice, and Flynn wanted to kiss her so very badly. He'd been waiting for her to make the first move, because he didn't want to seem too forward. Too much of the player everyone thought he was.

"Flynn?" she asked, swaying with him.

He closed his eyes and enjoyed the movement of her body, the scent of something clean and fruity about her. "Yeah, sweetheart?"

"Are you ever going to kiss me?" He stilled, and she laughed. "Got you with that one, didn't I?"

He looked down at her, not an ounce of teasing in him at the moment. "I've been waiting for you to kiss me," he said. "I didn't want to go too fast."

"Oh, in that case." She reached up and swept his cowboy hat right off his head. He normally didn't like anyone touching his hat, but the way Jessie held it with reverence as she gazed at him, all sorts of soft things in her eyes, Flynn didn't mind so much.

She ran her free hand through his hair, and Flynn closed his eyes again, his synapses firing on all cylinders. The woman knew how to drive him crazy, that was for sure.

Curling her fingers around the back of his neck, she balanced, and he felt her moving closer, closer, closer. Finally their lips touched, and Flynn growled in the back of his throat.

He held her tight, one arm hooked around her waist, and the other coming up to her face. Kissing her was unlike any other kiss he'd had, and Flynn's pulse romped through his chest as he enjoyed the best kiss of his life.

She pulled away far too soon, but Flynn let her. She kept herself right beside him, the only space between them near their faces. "Did you hear from the bank?" she whispered.

"Yes," he said. "They called this morning. I got approved."

"That's great," she said, her voice bright.

It was great. But not as great as kissing Jessie, so he dipped his head and did that again.

HALF AN HOUR LATER, SHE SAID, "I HAVE TO GO FEED THAT calf that won't eat without me."

"You do?" He kissed her again. "Are you sure?"

"Yes," she said as she giggled, his lips moving to her throat. "You behave yourself. Surely you have work to do."

He did, and a lot of it. "Yeah," he said. "Clay texted a while ago about Inkblaster throwing his shoes again. We need to call Knox."

"Go on then, cowboy," she said, swatting at his chest.

Flynn met her gaze, and the moment between them sobered. He wanted to say all the things he felt for her, but he was sure they'd already been conveyed in the way he kissed her. "See you later, Jess."

"'Bye, Flynn."

He left the barn, pulling himself together so no one would know he'd just spent far too long kissing his girlfriend. She'd said she'd talk to Rhodes that evening, and that Flynn should just lay low for one more day.

One more day.

He could do that. He hoped.

In the stables, he found Clay standing with the tall, black horse that had only been at the ranch for a year. Rhodes loved this beast, but Flynn couldn't figure out why. He wasn't all that nice, and he constantly seemed to cause trouble.

"Did you get in touch with Knox?" he asked Clay.

"Yeah, he's out at Fern Hollow this morning, but he said he'd come in this afternoon."

"Great." Flynn looked at the horse, who just glared right

back at him. "This one's wild," he said. "What should we do with him?"

"He just seems to have a love affair with kicking the wall," Clay said. "I've patched up more stalls than I can count."

"Maybe he needs to be outside at night," Flynn said.

"Rhodes will never agree to that," Clay said. "Doesn't trust the coyotes."

"We haven't had too many scares this year," Flynn said.

"Morning, boys," Rhodes said as he entered the stables. "What's goin' on now? Jess said something about calling Knox?"

"Your precious horse won't wear shoes," Flynn said. Rhodes stood there and appraised the horse, and dang if it didn't seem a little cowed by the other man's presence.

He reached toward the black beast and asked, "What are you doin', huh? They're just shoes. You've been wearing 'em your whole life." The horse pushed his nose against Rhodes's palm, and he said, "I'm taking him out."

"You're going to make him think he can kick a hole in his stall and then go for a ride," Flynn said.

Before Rhodes could argue—and he would argue—the door to the stables burst open. "Boss, there are six wolves already across the north fence." Monson Jackson stood there, his chest heaving and his face red.

"Wolves?" Flynn asked at the same time Rhodes said, "Saddle up. Clay, you and Flynn come with me on the ATV."

Flynn didn't argue. His heartbeat rioting in the back of his throat wouldn't let him anyway. Shep and Sally were out there, and Shep wouldn't be afraid to tangle with wolves.

He jogged behind Rhodes to the homestead, where the family owned a few ATVs. Several minutes later, they met up with his scouting team that had been out in the remote cabin last night.

"Status," Rhodes barked, but Flynn couldn't see anything.

Couldn't hear anything. Sometimes the vastness of the ranch scared him a little. Those wolves could be anywhere.

"Seven down, Boss," Gil said. "We pushed the wolves back and set up temporary fencing. They seem hungry though."

Hopefully, they weren't hungry for dogs.

"Okay," Rhodes said. "Let's wait for our backup team, and then we'll get them out and reinforce the fences. Clay, let's start moving the cattle west."

"On it," Clay said.

"It'll take three days to move the herd," Flynn said, stepping next to him, still scanning for any sign of movement.

"Yep," Rhodes said. "But I'm not losing seven a night by leaving them here." He glanced at Flynn. "What else should we do?"

"Call Wildlife Management," he said.

"I'm assuming Monson did that," Rhodes said.

"He did, Boss," Gil said, bending to pluck a piece of long grass and sucking on it. "Just heard on the radio that they're on their way."

"So we hold tight," Rhodes said. "Get our supplies out here. Move the herd. See what Wildlife Management says."

Flynn nodded, because he couldn't do anything else. The silence among the group suffocated him, and he pushed his hat back and then forward again. Words piled beneath his tongue, and he had to let them out.

"I may have broken my female fast a few days early," he blurted.

A smile spread across Rhodes's whole face. "I knew it." He pointed at Flynn with such joy in his eyes. "You owe me and Clay."

Flynn didn't care about the steak dinner, and he could barely meet his best friend's eye. "It's your sister."

Confusion puckered Rhodes's eyebrows. "What?"

"I started seeing your sister," he said.

"Cami has a boyfriend," Rhodes said.

"It's not Cami." Flynn walked away, half because he thought Rhodes might deck him. But why would he? Rhodes had never cared who his sisters dated in the past.

They didn't date players, Flynn thought, Rhodes's voice talking somewhere behind him.

Barking sounded, and Flynn turned toward it, his heart taking courage. Sure enough, Shep and Sally came streaking toward him, and they danced around him as he greeted them. At least they didn't care that he'd been out with far too many women in the past several years.

And they'd love the farm once Flynn got all the finances in order and could move in. Rhodes didn't say anything else about Jess as the Wildlife Management crew arrived. He was all business, and he and Flynn fired questions at the team to figure out how to make sure the wolves didn't cause a problem for the ranch again.

Flynn's phone chimed several times, and he ignored it until Rhodes said, "That's probably Jessie. I called her."

"You did?" Flynn yanked his phone out of his pocket, and Jessie's use of exclamation points wasn't done because she was happy. "I shouldn't have said anything. She said she was going to talk to you tonight."

"I don't care," Rhodes said. "You're a good man, Flynn. Maybe Jess'll help settle you down."

Flynn frowned at his phone. Did he need to be settled down?

Yes, a voice whispered in his head. And he definitely wanted Jess to be the one to do it. "Malcolm and Cami have the same age difference," he said. "I thought you'd be upset."

"I know you," Rhodes said. "And it's totally different."

Flynn wasn't sure how, but Rhodes barked something at another cowboy, and then they went back to the epicenter of the ranch, where Flynn still had a ton of work to do that day.

He rounded the corner of the barn though, watching the clouds gather in the sky as he dialed Jess.

"Hey," he said when she answered. "Don't be mad. Rhodes isn't."

"That's what he said," she said. "I just...we said I'd talk to him tonight."

"I may have forgotten," Flynn said with a smile. "My mind was all fogged up from kissing you."

She scoffed, the sound getting swallowed up inside her laughter. "You're impossible," she said.

"Impossible enough that you'll come to dinner with me tonight? *Not* at my place."

A few seconds of silence passed. "Yeah, all right," she said.

"Great," he said. "I'll pick you up when I leave the ranch."

CHAPTER NINE

The next week passed in a blur of activity around the ranch, kissing with Flynn in the barn and after work, and prep for the September cattle auction. The auctions were held every Wednesday, but Jessie only went to a couple in the fall.

She was already fielding calls from interested buyers, wanting to know when she'd be bringing the Quinn Valley Ranch cattle to the auction. She'd said, "First and third Wednesday in September, like always," at least a dozen times.

She did the auctions all at once, and it took over her life for most of August and September. She didn't mind, because it normally gave her something worthwhile to focus on. But now that she was dating Flynn, she found her waking hours full, full, full.

As August dawned, Rhodes came to her and asked her to help him ask Capri to marry him. "Of course," she said, glancing up from her standing desk in the barn. "What are you going to do?"

Capri worked at the grocery store now, and Rhodes let out a long sigh. "I'm going to build one of those soda can displays, spell something out." He looked at Jessie. "Is that a terrible idea?"

Jessie grinned at her brother. He hadn't said another word to her about dating Flynn, and as far as she knew, Flynn hadn't taken Clay or Rhodes out for that steak dinner. He hadn't bought his ranch back yet. Flynn hadn't been doing much of anything.

"I think it's great," she said. "I heard her talking about them at dinner on Sunday."

"She doesn't seem to like them, and I'll need a lot of help."

"I can sling boxes of soda around," Jessie said.

Rhodes grinned at her. "Great. We're doing it next week. I've asked a bunch of cowboys too." He didn't say Flynn, but Jessie knew he'd be there too. After all, Flynn was her brother's best friend.

"How are things going with you and Flynn?" Rhodes asked.

"Fine," Jessie said quickly, turning her back on her brother. "Just fine." She felt like clearing her throat, but she forced herself not to.

"I'm a little worried about him," Rhodes said.

"Yeah?" Jessie asked, twisting back to see that concern in Rhodes's eyes. "Why?"

"He closed on that ranch last week, and he hasn't moved yet."

"He closed on the ranch?" Jessie's eyebrows knocked right into her cowgirl hat. "Are you sure?"

"That's what he said last Friday."

It was Wednesday, and Jessie had asked him about the ranch over the weekend. It had seemed to take an extraordinarily long time to close, especially when the previous owners were already off the property.

"He told me it wasn't done yet," she said, her mind

churning on its own thoughts. "He said there was a delay, and he didn't know when he'd be able to move."

Their eyes met, and instant concern moved through Jessie too. "I'll ask him about it tonight. We're driving to Lewiston to see his mother."

Rhodes nodded and knocked on one of the posts nearby. "Tell her hello for me." With that, he left the calf barn, left Jessie with swirling ideas that didn't go down good roads.

Why wouldn't Flynn want to move back onto the ranch he'd lost when his father died? She'd been there with him when he'd looked at it, and he'd been nervous, sure. But he wanted the ranch. He'd always wanted that ranch back.

And if he'd closed last week, he had it.

She returned to her desk, but she didn't pick up her pen nor did she look at the paperwork she'd been preparing for the calves she'd be taking to the auction in a month.

Her memories surged as she tried to find when he could've gone to town to sign papers for the ranch. She'd never bought a house, but she'd listened to Georgia talk about how long it had taken Logan to sign all those papers when he'd bought the ranch where she'd live with him after they got married.

"It took two hours," Georgia had said.

Jessie didn't keep tabs on Flynn every moment of every day. But wouldn't she know if he left the ranch for hours?

"Apparently not," she muttered to herself, her mood souring by the moment. In the end, she left her paperwork unfinished and left in search of Flynn.

She found him brushing down a beautiful palomino in a pasture, his whistling alerting her to his position before she could see him. He sounded like a bird from an animated movie, and Jessie couldn't help smiling as she approached.

"Hey," he said, smiling at her. Oh, that smile. Jessie leaned against the fence as her stomach fluttered.

"How's Clover?" she asked.

"Oh, she's acting up," Flynn said. "Wouldn't do her rounds in the ring, so I brought her out here and told her she'd have to be in the pasture with the pigs for a while."

"She doesn't seem to care," Jessie said.

Flynn chuckled as he brushed. "No, she doesn't."

Jessie watched him work, those strong hands moving across Clover's side. She didn't know how to bring up the ranch without seeming pushy or accusatory.

"What are you up to?" he asked, glancing at her again. "We're not leaving for another hour or so, right?"

"Right," she said, sighing. "Just getting some sun."

"You hate the sun." Flynn slowed his motion. "Tell me what's going on."

She wasn't sure if she should be glad Flynn knew so much about her or annoyed. "Rhodes told me—"

"Oh, I hate sentences that start like that." Flynn glared at her and went back to the horse.

Jessie drew a deep breath and tried again. "You closed on the ranch last week, and yet when I asked you about it, you said there was a delay."

"No," Flynn said. "I said there was a delay in when I would be moving. Which is one-hundred percent true." He looked at her, his eyes dark in the shadows of his cowboy hat.

"Why don't you want to move to the ranch?" Jessie made her voice as gentle as possible. "I thought you wanted the ranch."

"I do," he said. "I'm just...." He exhaled. "I don't know, Jess."

"Okay," she said, her voice much too high. She and Flynn had been dating for almost two months, and she hadn't been keeping track of his previous girlfriends for very long, but she knew that was longer than anyone in the past year.

He didn't commit to women.

Or, apparently, ranches.

"I'll see you in a bit." She turned and walked away, her heart trembling in her chest with every step.

"Jess," Flynn called after her, and she paused, gathering her wits about her.

She turned back to him. "Yeah?"

"Can we go by my place before we go up to Lewiston?"

"Of course," she said. "Just let me know when you're ready to go. I'm going to go back to the homestead and cool off. You're right. I don't like the sun."

It made her freckles pop out and her hair turn redder, both things she didn't like. Plus, she still had to wrap the gift she'd bought for Flynn's mother.

He didn't say anything else, and Jessie walked back to the homestead with the heat of the sun burning her shoulders. She wished it would burn the doubts out of her mind too.

LATER, SHE BOUNDED DOWN THE STEPS TO FLYNN'S TRUCK, where both of his dogs hung over the side so she could pat them. "Hey, guys," she said, grinning at them. "Hey, did you have a good day on the ranch? I bet you did."

She got in the passenger side and glanced at Flynn. He had one arm draped over the steering wheel, that sexy smile on his face. He probably thought that grin could fix every-thing—and he wasn't far off.

"What's that?" he asked, nodding to the package in her hands.

"Chocolate covered raisins," she said. "You said your mother loved them."

"She does." He flipped the truck into reverse. "She's going to like you more than me."

Jessie laughed and shook her head, glad she'd been able to iron out the ponytail bump in her hair. "I doubt that, Flynn."

He rumbled down the dirt lane to the highway that led back to town before he spoke. "All right. Let's talk about the ranch."

"You talk," she said. "I don't have anything to say." She normally slid across the seat and rode next to him in the truck, her fingers laced through his, but today, she stayed on her side. Maybe she needed space to think. Maybe he needed space to talk. Maybe both.

"I closed on the ranch last Wednesday," he said. "I said I had to go with Knox out to Quinn Organics, which is totally true." He glanced at her. "I just didn't come back to the ranch afterward. It took forever, and I wished you were there the whole time."

Bitterness clawed its way up her throat. But she hadn't been there, because he hadn't told her. Something stung way down deep inside her. Why didn't he want to share his life with her?

Would he ever want to open himself up like that to someone? Why not her?

A sob caught in her mouth, and he looked at her. "I'm sorry, sweetheart."

"No," she said, shaking her head, unaware of when she'd started crying. "I—you—why didn't you tell me? We should be doing things together, Flynn. That's what people do."

"I know."

"Then why didn't you tell me? I wasn't doing anything Wednesday. I would've come with you, and helped you, and we could've celebrated with tacos and ice cream afterward."

Flynn shook his head, his jaw tight.

"You just signed and went home and sat on the porch with the dogs, didn't you?" She didn't mean to sound so demanding, but she deserved to know why Flynn had refused to include her in his life, especially when he had before.

"Something like that," he muttered to the windshield.

Jessie had a lot to say, but it all stayed stuffed up in her chest. Flynn kept his mouth shut and the truck moving, the awkwardness in the cab so thick Jessie could feel it between her fingers.

"I—maybe I shouldn't go to Lewiston tonight," she finally said.

"She's expecting you," Flynn said.

"So you just tell her we broke up," Jessie snapped. "It won't be the first time you've cut a woman loose."

The air hissed out of Flynn, and he pulled over to the side of the road quickly, causing Jessie to yelp and brace herself against the dashboard.

She looked at him, his anger sparking like lightning. "That's not fair," he said. "I told you why I did that, and you —you're the only one—" He shook his head, his chest heaving.

"I'm sorry," she said quickly. "Flynn, I didn't mean that. I just—why won't you share your life with me?" The blasted tears came back. "Why haven't you packed a single box? Why didn't you ask all the cowboys at the ranch to come help you move over the weekend?"

"Because," he said, his voice exploding out of him. "Because, then I have to go back to that place by myself. And I don't—I'm not sure I can go back there by myself."

"Flynn," she said, almost desperate for him to understand. "If you would have *told* me, you wouldn't have to do anything by yourself." She didn't care that she'd just laid out all of her feelings for him. If she expected him to do so, she would have to as well.

CHAPTER TEN

Flynn couldn't figure out how to put his feelings into words. They didn't make sense to him, so how in the world would they make sense to Jessie?

Everything inside him felt wound so tight, and he could barely breathe through the pressure against his lungs. He couldn't believe she'd just told him to break up with her.

He didn't want to break up with her—and that alone was enough to confuse him for days. When things got hard, Flynn did cut ties. No strings. The end.

Yet, somehow, he didn't want to do that with Jessie.

He didn't want to live on that ranch without someone there with him. He didn't want to leave Quinn Valley, where all of his friends were, where he'd been accepted, where he belonged.

"I'm sorry," he said again. "I...don't know what I'm doing."

"Obviously," she said, folding her arms and accompanying the harsh word with a soft smile.

Some of the tension in his shoulders bled out, and he relaxed. His eyes moved back out the windshield, the summer sunshine belying how stormy he felt inside.

"If I move to the ranch," he said. "I have to leave Quinn Valley."

"Yeah," Jessie said.

"And that means I don't get to kiss you in the barn in the morning, or see any of my friends, and I don't know." He let out a long sigh. "I want the ranch. I do. I went into a huge amount of debt to get it. But I…don't know. I don't—haven't been able to work out leaving Quinn Valley and being on my own."

"Flynn." She unbuckled her seatbelt and slid across the seat, pressing right into his side. He lifted his arm around her shoulders, enjoying her companionship, the very real presence of her, her calming spirit.

"Flynn," she said again, and he looked at her.

"You're beautiful," he said.

"Don't distract me." She smiled at him, but her eyes remained serious. "You can build everything we have at Quinn Valley at your own place. Everything."

"Yeah." He could, and he had access to Rhodes, who'd tell him everything he needed to know. And it wasn't like he'd be moving very far—his ranch sat on the west side of Quinn Valley, a mere thirty minutes from where he worked now.

"What did you decide to name it?" she asked.

"I don't know," he said, so tired of those three words.

"I don't believe that." She turned to him and swept her lips across his cheek. "Come on, cowboy. This doesn't sound like you at all, Flynn." Her last words were whispered, so full of emotion and truth.

"I know," he said. "I'm thinking of naming it Four Lanterns." He hoped she wouldn't ask why, but then she wouldn't be the Jess Quinn he knew.

"Why's that?"

He smiled to himself and said, "One for each member of my family. We've always been a light in the darkness for each other." He looked down at her again, easily matching his mouth to hers in a sweet, sweet kiss.

So much sighed through him, and he pulled away with the words, "So we're okay, right, Jess?" He leaned his forehead against hers. "I need you."

"Yeah," she said. "We're okay. We better get going, so your mother doesn't start to worry."

Flynn picked up his hat from where it had fallen during the kiss and put it back on his head, the weight of things already settling back on his shoulders. "Yeah," he said.

He drove them to Lewiston, where his mother received them with laughter and smiles. Flynn was right about how she reacted to Jess's gift, and she ushered them both inside where she had dinner waiting on the stove.

"She's lovely," his mother said, crowding him at the kitchen sink while he filled glasses with water.

"Ma," he said, setting down one glass and reaching for another. "Don't embarrass me." He smiled at her, and she swatted his arm.

"Please. But you haven't brought anyone home in years. Since Sandra."

"I know, Mom." He turned and put the drinks on the counter next to the salad. "I have some other news, Mom." He somehow communicated to Jess that he needed her, because she came to his side and put her hand in his, squeezing tightly.

"I bought back the farm." A measure of excitement moved through him, the same feeling that had been replaced by dread with every stroke of his signature.

His mother blinked at him, shock obvious on her face. "You did?"

"Yes," Flynn said. "I'm moving in this weekend. I'd like to have everyone come when I get the new signs done."

His mom turned to the stove, but all the burners had been turned off. "That's great, Flynn."

"You don't sound like it's great." He took a step and looked down at her. "What's wrong?"

"Nothing," she said.

"Mom."

"I don't want to go back to the farm," she said boldly.

"You don't have to," Flynn said, his own shock coloring his tone. "You can't come for dinner?"

"Yeah, I can come for dinner." She drew in a deep breath. "It's just, that's where your father died, and I don't—I'm glad I was able to sell it."

Flynn fell back a step, wishing his mother hadn't said that. "I grew up expecting to have it for my family." He didn't like this new spotlight on the darkness in his soul.

His mom deflated, and she cut a glance at Jessie. "I know that, dear. I know losing it was difficult. I'm sorry." She moved over to the counter with one step. "Let's say grace and eat."

Flynn did what she asked, but he couldn't help stewing over her words at dinner. She didn't feel bad about selling the farm, and all these years, he thought she had.

Jessie carried the conversation, something she was very good at, and Flynn let her. He drove her home and kissed her, mourning that he only had a few more days out on this ranch with her.

He said nothing though, because all of his doubts and fears were rising again. He didn't know what to do with all of them, but he did know he'd spoken at least one true thing that day.

He did need Jessica Quinn—badly.

❄

"ALL THIS STUFF IS READY?" RHODES ASKED AS SOON AS HE'D come into Flynn's living room. Flynn stood and surveyed the furniture he'd wrapped in sheets and the boxes he'd managed to pack in the last couple of days.

"Just the boxes," he said. "I'm leaving the furniture. My real estate agent will come stage the place once I'm gone." Flynn glanced around, thinking of all the work he needed to do. Windows to be washed. Floors scrubbed. Air freshened. He'd have to keep up with the yard too, though he was already planning on coming back to help Widow Jones every Saturday morning.

"All right, boys," Rhodes said as Clay and Wyatt came inside. "Get the boxes. Newt, help Flynn make some more boxes. I don't think he's as ready as he thinks he is." He grinned at Flynn, but the gesture didn't make Flynn feel better.

Working with his friends, he managed to get everything into the back of a few pickup trucks and out to the ranch he now owned.

"Twin Sisters," Wyatt said as he got out and started gazing around. "You keeping that?"

"No," Flynn said. "I'm going to name it Four Lanterns. I'll work on a sign in my free time."

Wyatt chuckled. "I don't think you're going to have much of that, bro."

"Much of what?" Clay asked, looking up at the house. "This place is awesome, Flynn." He took the stairs two at a time and opened the front door. A whistle of appreciation followed, and Wyatt followed Clay.

Flynn grabbed a couple of boxes from the back of his truck before he went in the house, and even he'd forgotten how nice it was.

"Wow," Wyatt said. "This is incredible. Someone spent a lot of time and money in here."

"Completely remodeled," Flynn said. "Though my bedroom was the first door on the left there."

"Yeah?" Clay smiled and went down the hall to poke his head inside. "Nice."

"There aren't many animals here," Flynn said. "Eight or nine horses. A flock of chickens. It's not a cattle ranch."

"And yet you said you don't have time to work at Quinn Valley," Rhodes said, also carrying boxes with him.

"I might have to come back part-time," Flynn said. "I just need some time off."

"Come back for the harvest," Rhodes said. "You'll be settled by then, and we'll need all the help we can get."

"I'll have to harvest here too," Flynn said. "That's all farmers do, didn't you know? Plant, cultivate, and harvest."

"I'm aware," Wyatt said, as he was primarily responsible for the crops at Quinn Valley.

Flynn did need time to take stock of everything at his new place, and he had enough money to last a few months while he did. After that, he sure hoped the Washburns had planted enough crops to turn a profit this year.

It didn't seem to take nearly as long to get the boxes inside the homestead as it had to get them out of his little brick house in town. And before he knew it, Rhodes clapped him on the shoulder and said, "I'm going to miss you at the ranch, Flynn."

Flynn grabbed onto his best friend and hugged him, glad when Rhodes didn't act weird about it. "I can do this, right?" he asked.

"Of course you can." Rhodes stepped back, a smile on his face. "You can do this, Flynn, and you can do it well." He walked toward the front door. "I'm going to go grab burgers from The Bacon Boys and bring them back. Jess said she'd be at your old place about four."

"Right," Flynn said, watching everyone walk out. They'd

be back, with food, and Flynn grabbed onto that comforting thought as he started to unpack the boxes.

The Washburns hadn't taken all of the furniture with them, so quick was their departure and so small was their place in Virginia. The couches and chairs in the dining and living room were of much better quality than Flynn had in the brick house, and he had a soft bed already set up to sleep in that night.

"Things are fine," he told himself, finishing with his plates, bowls, and cups. Leaving the rest of the boxes for now, he took the journey down the hall, stopping just inside his childhood bedroom.

It didn't hold the unmade bed, the dirty clothes, or the dresser full of baseball trophies anymore. Only a treadmill, with a television mounted on the wall in front of it. He probably wouldn't use that, as he had nine hundred acres of property to roam and explore and memorize.

Down the hall sat his sister's bedroom, and this one did have a queen-sized bed in it, with a dresser and frilly yellow curtains on the window. Across the hall sat a bathroom, and next to that a laundry room, with the back door that led into the garage and then into the yard.

In the back corner of the house sat his new master bedroom, with a bathroom almost the same size as it. Everything seemed to drip with prestige and money, and Flynn didn't wholly hate it.

He knew it wasn't the same bed, but he stood looking at the spot where his father had died all those years ago. He pressed one hand to his heart as he allowed himself to miss his dad more keenly than he had in a long, long time.

"I love you," he whispered, finally feeling that ache close somewhat. He didn't think it would ever be truly gone, but at least it didn't feel like it could open up and swallow him whole at any given time.

He squared his shoulders. "I'm meant to be here." And he felt a cleansing, washing tingle slide over his head, his shoulders, down his back.

And he knew.

God had just confirmed to him that yes, he was supposed to be on this farm, at this time.

"Thank you, Lord," he whispered, turning to start unpacking his clothes.

Only a few minutes later, the front door opened, and Rhodes called, "Food's here, Flynn."

CHAPTER ELEVEN

Jessie arrived early to Flynn's red brick house, her bucket of cleaning supplies full and ready to be put to good use. She'd managed to convince Georgia, Betsy, Cami, and Capri to come help her, and she'd promised them all cheesecake afterward. She already had Ivy, Bethany, and Maggie at the pub on alert.

It would be a regular Quinn dessert festival once they got this place cleaned up.

With everyone out of their cars and heading for the house, she did too. "All right," she said. "Jenny wants to list this place on Monday, and I told her it would be ready."

She opened the door, not sure what to expect. But furniture wrapped in sheets, and trash on the floor, and a half-dead plant still in the kitchen window wasn't it.

"I'll start in the kitchen," she said, smothering a sigh. She felt like billing Flynn for the cheesecake she'd have to provide her sisters for doing this for her.

"I'll take the bathrooms," Betsy said.

"Bedrooms," Georgia said, following Betsy and her bucket of cleaning supplies.

"I'll stay out here," Capri said, toeing an empty box of crackers that looked like it had been smashed under the couch. "And go out into the yard when I'm done here."

"I'll work on the front porch," Cami said. "And do the windows."

Soon enough, the scent of bleach and lilacs replaced that of Flynn's cologne and leather and dirty boots. The vacuum cleaner ran, and in only a couple of hours, everything sparkled and shone and smelled great.

"He didn't take his rocking chair," she said, wiping the sweat from her forehead as she stepped back out onto the front porch. "I wonder if he wants it."

"He's here," Capri said from her spot in the front flowerbed, weeds covering the ground at her feet. "So you can ask him."

"Thanks, everyone," Jessie said, suddenly anxious for them to leave. She hugged her sisters and Capri, and they started filing down the steps and to their cars.

"You guys came and cleaned?" Flynn asked, watching them.

"Heya, Flynn," Betsy said. "Looks good in there now."

"I'm embarrassed," he said. "I didn't clean up at all."

"We saw," Georgia deadpanned, a smile on her face.

Flynn looked at Jessie, and he didn't look entirely pleased. "They wanted to come help," Jessie said. "We all love you, Flynn."

She pulled in a tight breath at the words, but they were true. She loved Flynn on a brotherly level for sure. If they hadn't been dating, she'd have missed him on the ranch. Felt his loss, the same way her sisters did.

Stepping into his arms, she drew his attention fully to her. "Don't be mad," she said, tipping up to kiss him. Someone honked as they drove away, and she heard feminine laughter.

She didn't care, because kissing Flynn was everything she'd ever hoped and imagined it would be.

"Come on," she said a minute later. "Take me out to Four Lanterns and show me around."

BY THE TIME JESSIE SHOWED UP AT THE PUB, THE QUINN dessert party was in full swing. Cami sat next to Ivy and Maggie, saying, "At least you guys have someone. I can't seem to find someone to date for longer than a couple of weeks."

"Riley's was a week, and look at her," Maggie said knowingly. "You just need to find the right guy."

"Yeah." Cami sighed as Jessie sat next to Maggie. "Hey, there you are."

"Yeah, sorry, I went with Flynn for a minute." Those words seemed to bring everyone's attention to her, and Jessie didn't like the weight of it.

In that moment, she realized she liked being on the sidelines, out of the spotlight, taking care of the calves at her standing desk in the barn.

Her cousins were great, though she heard all the questions before even one was vocalized.

"Yes," she said. "I'm dating Flynn Hollister."

"And how's it going?" Cami asked, though she knew full well how Jessie's relationship with the handsome cowboy was going.

"Great," she said airily. "He's moved off the ranch now, and he has a lot of work to do at his new farm. But good." She reached for the last piece of cheesecake. "This is mine, right?"

"I saved it for you," Ivy said, sliding the plate closer to her. "And I'm glad you're seeing Flynn. You two are cute together."

"Which one is Flynn?" Maggie asked.

"The super-hot one?" Cami asked. "Been single forever. Loves to dance...." She raised her eyebrows, and Jessie was glad she hadn't finished that sentence.

"Oh, right. Flynn." Maggie smiled at Jessie. "He doesn't usually have girlfriends for long either, Cami, and look at him now."

"Yeah, there's totally hope for you," Ivy said, turning back to Cami and taking the spotlight off Jessie. Thankfully.

They started talking about the cowboys they could set Cami up with, and Jessie ate entirely too much sugar, first in the form of cheesecake, and then a blondie, and then mint chocolate chip ice cream.

Later, as she drove past Granny's cabin on the way back to the homestead, she whispered, "Start praying, Granny. I think Flynn and I are going to need it."

A WEEK PASSED WITHOUT FLYNN AT THE RANCH, AND THEN another. Jessie missed him more than she thought possible, and she knew now why Georgia and Betsy didn't spend nearly as much time at home as they used to.

They wanted to be with the men they loved, and they wore the diamonds that allowed them to do that.

Jessie felt like she had to ask Flynn if she could come see him in the evenings, and she invited him to the ranch for Sunday lunches and dinners, though those things would all change once Betsy wasn't living in the homestead anymore.

A couple of weeks before the first auction date, she climbed the steps to his homestead, feeling weary and worn out. She knocked, but he didn't answer the door, and she sat on the top step in the shade, wondering what she was doing.

In all honesty, she felt like she was pushing Flynn into a corner he didn't want to be in. They did text a lot, but it was mostly about work, and he hadn't asked her about the auction once. When he'd worked on the ranch, he stopped by every morning and talked to her about the calves, the bid sheets she was preparing, the weights of the cows she'd selected.

Now he had his own animals to care for, and fences to fix, and crops to work on. Since the farm had sat without any human care for over a month, he did have a lot of work to do. She didn't begrudge him that. Flynn had always worked long hours, and they'd found time to talk, go to dinner, and spend time together.

But he'd stopped coming to church too, and Jessie actually felt lonely again.

She scoffed at herself and watched as a line of dust lifted into the air to her right. Sally emerged around the corner, and Jessie clapped her hands as if the dog didn't already know she was there.

The cattle dog came right up to her and licked her face while Jessie patted her. "Where's Flynn, huh? What's he doing?"

He'd said she could come that night, and she expected seven-thirty to be plenty late for him to come in from his chores. Maybe something had happened. Jessie knew the perils and unpredictability of a ranch better than anyone.

Several minutes later, an unfamiliar truck came roaring down the road in the same direction Sally had come from. Jessie stared at it, blinking a couple of times before her mind accepted that it was painted a light pink.

It came all the way to the homestead and parked next to her white one, and a curly-haired blonde jumped from behind the wheel. She was perky and petite, and everything Jessie could never be. She wore a pair of jeans that seemed welded to her legs, and a red shirt that actually had a knot tied on the side near her hip, the way women much younger than her did.

She obviously didn't see Jessie, because she emitted a

high-pitched, girly giggle when Flynn got out of the truck too.

"Contract's inside," he said, moving toward the house. "Come on in, Francine. You can sign it and come back tomorrow."

Jessie stood just as Flynn reached the shadows cast by the house, her heart thumping everywhere but in the right spot inside her body.

"Jess," Flynn said, surprise clear in his voice, as if he wasn't expecting her.

He forgot, she told herself as he climbed the steps. He didn't touch her the way she expected him to. "I just hired Francine to be my mechanic."

"Oh," Jessie said, sure the giggling woman had more on her mind that a tune-up of Flynn's tractors, though he had mentioned that almost all of the equipment was old and in need of repair.

Flynn smiled at her and went right past, opening the door and leaving it open for everyone to follow him inside. The dogs did, and Francine came leaping up the stairs like a little puppy dog herself.

She didn't even say hello to Jessie. She just went past her, the smile slipping a little bit. Jessie felt like she'd been wrapped in waxed paper. She could hear voices in Flynn's house. See the landscape before her, including that ridiculous pink pickup.

But nothing was all the way clear, nothing made enough sense. Her only thought screamed at her to get away from this blurred reality. Find some clarity. Figure things out.

She heard her footsteps as she went down the wooden stairs to the packed earth. Heard the rumble of her engine as it started. Heard her heart cracking as she drove away from Flynn and Four Lanterns Farm.

She'd eaten too much fried cheese, bacon-and-cheese potato skins, and brownie skillets by the time Flynn found her at the pub.

"Hey," he said, sliding into the booth across from her the way he had weeks ago. "Why'd you leave?"

She lifted one shoulder into a shrug, because she didn't want to tell him the truth. The skillet was empty, a pool of melted vanilla ice cream still there, so she didn't have anything to distract her.

Nothing but the dreamy man in front of her. And she wasn't blind to his charms—every woman in the pub had looked his way when he'd come in.

"What's wrong?" he asked, reaching across the table to cover her hands with his.

"You hired Francine," Jessie said.

"I needed a mechanic," he said, confusion furrowing his brow. "We talked about it earlier this week."

"Yeah, when we talked about me bringing you dinner tonight so we could spend some time together."

Understanding filled his eyes, and he ducked his head. His sudden realization didn't make anything better. In fact, the fact that he'd forgotten she was coming made everything worse.

"It's fine." Jessie sighed the words out and slid out of the booth. "I have to get home."

"Jess," he said, following her, though he was obviously annoyed with her.

She stalled at the end of the table, not wanting to cause a scene in her cousin's pub. Too many eyes here. Too many people who knew every member of her family and would be talking before she got to her truck.

"I feel like I'm forcing you to see me," she said. "And I

hate that." She threw some money on the table and left the pub, desperate to get away from everyone and everything. She hadn't thought about leaving the ranch since poker night months ago, but now anywhere felt better than staying here.

"Jess, you're not forcing me to do anything," he said.

"I know," she said. "And I hate that too."

"You hate that you're not forcing me to do things?" Flynn caught up to her a few steps from her truck and touched her arm. "Can you wait, please?"

She turned toward him, feeling two seconds away from exploding. "I don't see you anymore," she said. "Not at the ranch, which is fine. But I beg you to come to your place, and then when you finally say yes, you're there with another woman."

"She's a mechanic," Flynn said.

"Right," Jessie said. "Did she actually fix anything? Because I have my doubts about Francine." Her chest heaved, and she suddenly had so many reservations about everything. "And you don't come to church anymore. And you don't come to lunch at the homestead, and I don't know, Flynn. Maybe this just isn't going to work."

"Because I'm trying to put my farm together?"

"Maybe we should just take a break for a while, until your life is more settled. Until you know what you want to commit to."

"Oh, I see." He chuckled, but the sound didn't hold much happiness. "You think I can't commit to you."

"To anything," Jessie said.

"You're so wrong," he said, taking a step closer to her. "I'm committed to my farm."

Jessie waited for him to say more. She couldn't blame him for making a living. She knew the pressures of running a ranch.

"I have to go," Jessie said. "The auction is tomorrow, and

I'm tired already." She got behind the wheel and gave Flynn an extra second to stop her. Lean into the window and tell her he was committed to her. To them.

Heck, she'd take a *good luck* about the auction.

She got nothing.

CHAPTER TWELVE

Flynn surveyed the line of tractors parked in the equipment shed, none of which would start. He had no idea what to do about any of them, and Francine had been there all morning, and she didn't either.

He now had his doubts about Francine, who lounged in the back of his truck like she was a model waiting for the photographer to show up.

So Jessie had been right.

Flynn sighed and turned around. "All right, Francine," he said. "Who do you know that's a real mechanic?"

"I think you just need new tractors," she said, hopping down from the pickup.

"No." Flynn shook his head. "Let's get you back to your car, and you can go on back to the nail salon or wherever you came from." Then he'd escape to the air conditioned homestead and try to figure out how to hire good help.

Rhodes managed to do it, and Flynn needed to call his best friend. Maybe Jonas Penshaw could work at Quinn Valley and here at Four Lanterns.

He loathed the idea of getting in the cab with Francine,

but he couldn't leave her out here by herself. The drive back to the dirt in front of the house happened quickly, and Flynn practically flew from the truck, the image of Joseph fleeing from Potiphar's wife in his mind.

"Thanks so much," he said, nodding at Francine as he hurried toward the front door.

"You're going?" she asked, darting in front of him.

"Yes," he said, drawing in a deep breath. "It's not going to work out, Francine. You have a great day."

She put one hand on his chest, and Flynn's skin crawled. "Are you sure?"

"So very sure." He stepped back, out of her reach, and added, "I have a girlfriend."

She giggled. "Okay. So do lots of my boyfriends. And your ranch is so far away, and...."

"Nope," he said.

Anger flashed across her face. "Fine. But you're not fooling anyone, Flynn Hollister. Everyone in town knows you don't actually keep girlfriends." She stomped over to her car and drove away.

Everything pinched inside Flynn, but he managed to make it up the stairs and inside the house. Safely behind the closed and locked front door, he exhaled.

"I do too keep girlfriends," he said to the empty house, pulling his phone out of his back pocket. Jessie's line rang and rang, and sharp disappointment cut through him when he got her voicemail instead of her.

She was probably screening, and that thought poisoned his mind.

"Wondering if you wanted to go to dinner tonight," he said. "After the auction. Call me." He hung up quickly, because duh. She was at the auction today. No wonder she hadn't answered.

"And you were going to go," he reminded himself. A glance

at the clock told him if he wanted to be at the cattle auction in time to bid on the Quinn Valley cows, he had to leave right that minute.

His stomach protested against the idea, but he grabbed his wallet and headed back out the front door. The cattle auction took place at the fairgrounds, and while Four Lanterns wasn't so far away, as Francine had said, it still took ten minutes to get back to civilization. And another ten to get to the auction.

When he walked in, the auctioneers voice ran ten miles a minute, and it took Flynn a few extra seconds to comprehend what the man was saying.

He caught "Quinn Valley" and slaughterhouse, and hoped he hadn't missed the calves Jessie always brought to increase herd size and ensure genetic lines didn't die out.

The auction ended as he took a seat, his paddle in his hand.

"Up next, we have three hundred head of yearlings from Quinn Valley Ranch. These can be used to increase population or you can bring 'em back next year and sell 'em for slaughter."

Flynn perked up. These were the cows he wanted. The starting price was high, but Quinn Valley was well-known for their quality stock. A couple of other people bid before Flynn threw his number into the running.

One person dropped out, and he caught sight of Jessie's reddish-blonde ponytail swing to try to catch a glimpse of him. He ducked behind the tall cowboy in front of him and bid again, finally winning the three hundred calves.

He'd have to talk to her eventually, and she'd know he'd just bought her cows the moment she checked out. But for now, he dashed out of the room the moment the auction ended, handed in his paddle, and hurried outside.

Adrenaline rushed through him, as did a measure of

sadness. He should've been here all day with Jessie. Asked her what she needed help with, and how he could support her.

The work on his own farm had stolen his attention. It wasn't a bad thing to be focused on, he knew that. He just didn't want it to be the *only* thing—and the farm had become the only thing.

I'm sorry, he tapped out to Jessie, right as a text from her came in.

I can't go to dinner tonight. I'll be at the auction house all night.

She might as well have added a, *Just like I told you, Flynn*, to the sentence. Foolishness filled him, and he stalled in his apology to her. If she was texting him, she'd listened to her message. Her auctions were over.

He'd never paid much attention to the auctions, but he knew she prepped for them for weeks and months. She'd be tired tonight, and he should have dinner ready for her.

He looked at the apology he'd been about to send, quickly changing it to, *Okay. What time will you be done tonight?*

I don't know.

Maybe I could bring you dinner whenever you're done.

It took several minutes for her next text to come in. *I don't think so, Flynn.*

The breath left his body, and he hated texting out important conversations. He tapped the phone icon and listened to her line ring and ring and ring.

I'm busy, she texted. *I don't think you need to worry about us anymore, Flynn. I told you that yesterday. We need a break.*

Humiliation hit him hard in the chest. "A break?" Sure, she'd said that last night, but he'd told her he was committed to his farm. He could commit to things. People. He could.

Are you breaking up with me over a text?

He wished he could recall the message the moment he touched his thumb to the green arrow to send it.

Yes, her message said. *I have to go. Sorry, Flynn.*

"Sorry, Flynn," he repeated. Was she really sorry?

He looked up, his eyes finding the door to the auction house easily. No one went in or out, and when his phone chimed again, he really didn't want to look at it.

In the end, he did, because how did someone ignore a text when they knew they had one? Thankfully, or maybe not, it wasn't from Jessie. The text had a link where he could pay for his cattle, and he tapped on it, about to spend thousands of dollars just to get Jessie to talk to him again.

She couldn't break up with him over a text. Not with their history. Not only had he been with her longer than any other woman in the past five years, they were friends.

Weren't they?

He typed in all the right numbers and sent the money flying through cyberspace from his account to hers. She arranged all the transport of cattle, and she'd be busy with that until next week's auction.

But at least he'd get to see her. If he could just tell her what he'd been so desperate to do at Four Lanterns. If she could just accept his apology.

With the payment made, surely Jess would find out who had won the auction any minute now. And then she'd text him back, and everything would be fine between them.

No texts came in. His heart beat louder and louder, quicker and quicker, and still she didn't call or text.

In the end, he had work to do, and he couldn't sit in his truck forever. So he backed out and called Rhodes.

"Hey," his friend said, pure cheer in his voice. "How are things going?"

"Not great," Flynn said. "What are the chances I could borrow Jonas for a few days?"

"Trouble with your machinery?"

"All of it," Flynn said, a sigh accompanying the words. He

drove by the little church he'd gone to with all the Quinns, pulling off quick enough to give himself mild whiplash.

"I'll send you his number," Rhodes said. "And Clay can come help too. He's not bad with a wrench."

"Great," Flynn said, trying not to be too excited to see other people he knew and cared about. "Thanks, Rhodes."

The call ended, and Flynn peered out the windshield at the spire on top of the church. There wasn't a single car in the parking lot, but Flynn got out of the idling truck and walked down the sidewalk to try the door.

Locked. Back in the cool, air-conditioned interior, he simply sat in the parking lot. "Sorry I haven't been to church," he said, his voice somewhat foreign in all this silence. "I've been real busy at the farm. There's so much that needs to be done."

A general sense of drowning overtook him, and he'd learned to breathe through that in the past month or so since moving onto the ranch. It seemed to take longer than usual to find his center, but he eventually did.

"Help me," he said. "I want the farm to be a family legacy again. But I've just lost the only woman I've seriously considered having a family with."

The heavens didn't open, and God didn't speak to him. But Flynn felt a sense of peace way down in the tips of his boots. "We're okay, right, Lord?" he asked.

Flynn hadn't been to church in a while, but he didn't go to church to snuggle with Jessie. He went to feel the Lord's hand in his life. He had missed it these past few weeks, but he still felt close enough to God to know he was loved.

And that yes, he and the Lord were okay.

Now, he just had to figure out how to make things okay with Jess.

CHAPTER THIRTEEN

Jessie held everything together until the end of the auction. She'd brought seven lots of cattle on Quinn Valley's first appearance at the weekly auction, and she'd done very well. Bidding wars in all the auctions, with half a dozen people chatting her up before the round with her cattle in it.

Rhodes would be thrilled, and her father would be proud.

Jessie should be happy, but she felt like throwing up. And crying.

Instead, she put a smile on her face, ignored the rolling in her stomach, and focused on the winners of the auction. The auction house made it easy to collect the money and communicate with the winner.

She knew most of them anyway. She'd been present in the auction, and there was only one where she hadn't caught a glimpse of the winning bidder.

"Papers for auction four," Grant said, handing her a few pages before he dashed off again.

"Thanks," she called after him, glancing at the top paper. Ah, here was her mystery buyer, and she hoped she wouldn't have to arrange transportation for three hundred head of cattle that was too far.

Her heart flipped when she saw the name on the paper.

"Flynn bought them?" She looked up, sure he'd be standing right there to tell her she couldn't read anymore. He wasn't, and the activity in the auction house meant no one else had even heard her.

Four Lanterns wasn't a cattle ranch, though with nine hundred acres, Flynn could certainly raise some beef—which he was obviously going to do. Quinn Valley beef.

Her first instinct was to pull out her phone and call him. Find out what he was doing. But she'd literally broken up with him via a text twenty minutes ago.

She couldn't talk to him right now, and she certainly didn't want to communicate with him about getting the calves from Quinn Valley to his farm. Her mind whirred with possibilities. She could ask Rhodes to do it. Or Grant, who always helped with the cattle.

But she didn't want to explain anything to anyone, least of all her brother or another cowboy on the ranch. Even her sisters would try to get her to tell them how she was feeling. And that was the problem. She didn't know how she was feeling.

What she knew was that Flynn had been distant since he'd signed the closing papers on his farm, and once he'd moved and started working the land he'd bought, he'd disappeared completely. Physically, mentally, emotionally.

Jessie had never thought of herself as a needy woman before, but when it came to Flynn, she certainly was. Stuffing away the thought, she simply put his paperwork on the bottom of her stack and focused on the conversation she'd been having with another buyer.

She couldn't ignore Flynn forever, but she could put him

off until she got to the safety of her bedroom in the homestead.

Hours passed before that happened, and Jessie was completely wrung out by that time. She hadn't eaten lunch because of the auction, and Betsy had left dinner for her on a plate on the kitchen counter. She couldn't eat that either, as her tears brimmed so close to the surface.

Her head swam, and she couldn't get a decent breath that wasn't filled with everything Flynn. She'd only felt this desperate and broken one other time—just before her birthday, months ago, when she'd considered leaving the ranch.

"Maybe I could do that," she said, her voice cracking on the last word just as she closed her bedroom door behind her. She leaned her head back, as if that would keep the tears from streaming down her face.

"You broke up with him," she told herself, the misery streaming through her evident in every syllable. She drew in a deep breath through her nose, trying to find something to hold onto.

"Jess?" Cami knocked on her door, and Jessie danced away from it, her heart booming out a staccato rhythm in her chest.

"Just a sec," she said, glad her voice didn't sound two beats away from dying. Her face flamed with her distress, and she wiped at her eyes. Thankfully, she wasn't wearing makeup, but she didn't think for one second that Cami wouldn't notice that she'd been crying.

She opened the door and turned back to her bed without looking at her sister.

"Hey, so Clay—" When Jessie turned, Cami cut off as if someone had muted her. "You've been crying." She came in and closed the door. "What's wrong? Did something go wrong at the auction?"

Jessie shook her head, unable to speak. She just lifted one

shoulder into a shrug and collapsed onto her bed. Everything felt so heavy, and she reminded herself that it had for a while now.

"It's Flynn then." Cami hurried across the room and sat next to Jessie on the bed. "It's okay, sissy. What happened?"

"He's just...unavailable." He'd been unavailable, off-limits, to her for years.

"Because of the farm?"

She nodded. "Yes, that. And he hired some woman who is *not* a mechanic, and then he bought all these calves, and asked me to dinner, and everything is a mess."

Cami put her arm around Jessie, and she leaned into her sister. "Hey, things must not be too messy if he asked you to dinner?"

"He only did it out of pity," Jessie said. "Because I got mad at him yesterday for forgetting I was bringing him a burger." She inhaled slowly, some rational thought entering her mind again. "I don't need him to pity me. And I'm done begging him to hang out with me." She was thirty years old, for crying out loud. Not sixteen.

"I'm sure he wants to see you," Cami said.

"I'm not sure of anything anymore," Jessie said. "It's fine." She reached back and took her hair out of the ponytail it had been caged in all day. She ran her fingers through it and shook her hair over her shoulders. "Now, you were saying something about Clay?"

"No," Cami said quickly. "Nope. Didn't say anything about Clay."

Jessie knew she'd heard her sister speak Clay's name, but she didn't want to think about her cute, petite younger sister going out with yet another man. Then Jessie would be last again, and she was so tired of feeling left out.

Left out of the family. Left out of conversations. Left out of wedding plans, and shopping trips, and everything.

"I'm going to bed," she said, knowing she wasn't being fair. She'd declined to go with Georgia and Betsy as they shopped for wedding dresses. "I have a bunch of things to do tomorrow to be ready for next week's auction."

"Hey, it's almost over," Cami said with a smile.

Jessie basked in the love and warmth from her sister. She and Cami had always been best friends, and she hugged her sister, the emotion welling up inside her again. "Thanks, Cami."

"Jess, maybe you just need to give him more time."

"Yeah," Jessie said, because she just wanted Cami to leave. She did, and Jessie changed into her pajamas and crawled into bed. "But he's already taken up so much of my time," she muttered to the ceiling. "Hasn't he, Lord? How much time do I give him?"

God didn't answer, but one of Jessie's favorite stories about the lost sheep came into her mind. The Lord wasn't satisfied with having ninety-nine out of one hundred. He wanted all of His sheep—including Flynn.

So the Lord had gone looking for him, leaving the others behind.

"Have you forgotten me?" she whispered, fresh tears coating her cheeks. In that moment, she knew she wasn't alone. She had not been forgotten by God.

Maybe just by Flynn.

THE FOLLOWING DAY, WHEN CLAY CAME INTO THE HAY barn, Jessie cornered him and said, "I need a favor."

"Uh oh," he said, searching her face. "What's this about?"

"I know you asked out my sister, and while she, uh, didn't have time to tell me everything, you totally owe me for that." Jessie lifted her chin, daring Clay to contradict her.

"Fine," he said, a sparkle in his eyes. "You're going to win this one, Jess. Just tell me what you need."

"I need you to arrange all the transportation for one auction. Just one." She stepped over to her standing desk and collected Flynn's paperwork. Clay would have questions, but she hoped the answers would be obvious.

"You want me to handle one of the auctions?"

"Sort of," she said. "The auction is done. Paid for. I just don't have time to arrange to move three hundred head of cattle."

He looked dubious, but he took the papers she handed him. "Jess, this is...." He looked up. "What happened with you guys?"

"He bought a farm and got busy," Jessie said. "It happens." She was so proud of herself that her voice didn't give away any of her hurt.

"Jess." Clay shook his head. "I'm sure that's not true."

"Flynn's always been ultra-focused on one thing," she said.

"Yeah." He looked at the papers again. "But Jess, that's always been you."

She didn't dare to hope he was right, though he was one of Flynn's best friends. "No," she said. "That's been him trying to hide how depressed he's been."

"Well, I don't have time for this either." Clay handed the paper back. "Three hundred head of cattle, Jess? That's a whole day's work."

"I know," she said. "That's why I can't do it."

"Well, I can't either. Without Flynn, we're drowning getting ready for Harvest Day. Rhodes just asked me to find more help."

Harvest Day. Flynn would be coming to the ranch for that. She'd have to see him. *There will be a lot of people there*, she told herself. Everything would be fine. She'd avoided him before; she could do it again.

He shook the paper, and Jessie had no choice but to take it back. "Sorry, Jess."

"Clay," she said, a bit of a whine in the tone. "I need you to do this for me. You owe me."

"You think so?" He squinted at her. "Because of you, I almost lost a date with her to Malcolm."

"Oh, please," Jessie said. "If you had asked when Malcolm did, you'd be out the door like he is, and he'd be primed to take my sister dancing." She lifted her eyebrows. "She was in no place for a new relationship at the time, trust me."

Clay still looked doubtful, but he took the paper from her again. "Fine, but you owe me now. Big time."

"How big time?"

"Next time you come to poker night, you have to coach me. Tell me all your secrets."

"Deal," Jessie said, shaking Clay's hand. He chuckled and walked out of the barn, and a slip of happiness moved through her.

But without Flynn in her life, the misery snuck right back in.

CHAPTER FOURTEEN

Flynn frowned at the texts from Clay. He arranged the transportation and delivery of the cattle he'd won at the auction, which meant Jess wouldn't be coming to the farm.

Disgusted, he didn't answer his friend.

He set bread in the toaster and dumped sugar by the spoonful into his coffee, his brain whirring through possibilities. Clay was decent with a wrench, and maybe he could take a look at just one tractor while he was here.

Instead of texting him back, he called Clay.

"Flynn," Clay said, and his voice sounded a little off. "What's up?"

"You're bringing the cattle?"

"Well, we have the Cattlemen's Corral bringing them. I just need to know a good day and time for delivery."

"Whenever," Flynn said. "I'm here all the time."

"How about next Tuesday?"

"Tuesday is fine," Flynn said. "So you won't be coming at all?"

"No," Clay said. "We're days behind on the Harvest Festival, and I got approval to hire this out."

Flynn started nodding as soon as Clay said no, though no one could see him. "Okay," he said. "I'll be here Tuesday."

"Rhodes mentioned you're having some mechanical issues," Clay said.

"Yes," Flynn said, but he was not going to ask Clay for help. Sure, he felt like he was drowning, especially without the ability to text Jessie and get a daily dose of oxygen. But he could figure things out. He could, and he would.

"I could come out on Saturday," Clay offered.

"No, you can't," Flynn said. "If you're really behind on the Harvest Festival, you can't."

"Yeah." Clay sighed. "I can't. But let me give you the name of someone who can come. He's great."

Flynn put his friend on speakerphone so he could type in the name and number of the mechanic Clay knew. "Thanks," he said.

"Good luck, Flynn."

The call ended, and Flynn exhaled heavily. He was grateful Clay hadn't asked about Jessie, though surely he knew. He wondered what she was telling people, but then again, he almost didn't want to know.

It didn't matter.

"Of course it matters," he told himself and the toast as it popped up. "This is Jessica Quinn we're talking about." His throat tightened, and he buttered his toast, trying to get everything inside him to settle down.

But it didn't. His emotions surged and roared and rushed through him. This was his Jess, and he needed her back in his life.

Then go get her back.

The thought moved swiftly through his mind, entirely not his own.

He put down the butter knife and reached for his keys and then his wallet. He wanted to trust God. He wanted to act on promptings.

He wanted Jessica Quinn.

The thirty-five minute drive from his farm to the ranch where he used to work took so long, despite Flynn driving over the speed limit. He turned onto the familiar lane, the row of cabins on the left-hand side of the road so comforting.

At this time of day, on a Thursday, he had no idea where Jess would be. She could literally be anywhere, including the homestead with all of her sisters. The truck she drove wasn't parked there though, and he turned right and headed out toward the barns.

Her truck wasn't anywhere, and Rhodes came out of the stables and saw Flynn before he could get off the ranch. He waved him down, and Flynn searched his mind for a reason he could be at the ranch.

"Hey," he said, rolling down the window.

"What are you doing here?" Rhodes took off his hat and wiped his hand through his hair.

Flynn smiled at him, because it felt good to have contact with the Quinns again. "I came out to see about the Harvest Festival," he said. "Clay said you guys were behind, and I thought maybe I could help for a few hours this afternoon."

"Don't you have a farm to run?" Rhodes asked with a grin.

"Yeah, well." Flynn shrugged.

"You came to see Jess," Rhodes said. "Just admit it."

"Nope," Flynn said, putting his truck in park and turning it off. "Now, point me in the right direction for whatever needs to be done for the Harvest Festival."

As Rhodes started explaining what needed to be done, Flynn had another great idea. He couldn't just waltz up to Jessie on the ranch—he didn't know what he'd been thinking trying that.

But he could get her to talk to him across the poker table. Before he did a single thing, he texted Betsy. *I need a favor. Can you give your poker spot to Jessie for next week?*

He'd only taken one step toward the far barn to make sure they had the twine they needed for the harvest when Betsy responded. *She won't take it.*

So she knew they'd broken up. Rhodes hadn't, though. *What can I do then?* Flynn looked at the words, feeling foolish and ridiculous. He was a grown man. He didn't run to his friends to make his relationships work.

Of course, he hadn't had a real relationship he cared about in years.

He deleted off the question and typed out, *I just want to talk to her.*

Then talk to her.

Flynn sighed. If only that were so easy. Like he'd always done over the years, he put his head down and got the work done. It wasn't the jobs that needed doing around his own land, but it was good work. Honest work. Work that kept his mind off of Jess—at least for a few seconds.

He didn't need to check out with Rhodes, and he wouldn't find him out on the ranch anyway. He knew his friend had been quitting earlier and earlier so he could spend time with his fiancée.

So when he'd finished the things Rhodes had asked him to do, he got behind the wheel of his truck and headed off the ranch. He hoped he'd see Jessie walking along the road, but he didn't. He didn't see anyone, and his stomach settled somewhere near his shoes once the tires hit asphalt.

"Did I make a mistake?" he asked himself. He'd wanted his farm since the moment he'd lost it. So why did he feel like he was leaving an important piece of himself at Quinn Valley Ranch?

HE MADE IT THROUGH FRIDAY AND ON SATURDAY morning, Clay's friend came out to the farm with him.

"You didn't have to come," Flynn said, shaking Clay's hand. "I know how much you guys have left to do for the festival."

"I'll get it done," he said. "This is Cole Compton, the mechanic I was telling you about."

Flynn shook the other man's hand too, liking that he had grease stains on his hands and a cowboy hat on his head. "I hope you're a miracle worker," he said. "Because I don't have a single machine that works and no money to replace them."

He probably should've spent the cash he had on operational equipment rather than three hundred head of cattle, but he couldn't undo the auction now. And he wanted those cows. He knew how to work a cattle ranch, but he had no idea what to do with a farm.

He'd learn, and he had all of his dad's records. He just needed more time to get settled, figure things out. No matter what, he knew he couldn't do any type of work around the farm without an operational tractor.

"Let's see 'em," Cole said. They all piled into Flynn's truck, and he drove down the lane to the equipment shed. It held a half a dozen tractors, and he opened the doors with the button as he explained.

"I don't know why I can't get any of them started. I've searched online. I have all the keys. This place was plowed and planted when I bought it, but I don't know how they did it."

The door rumbled up and up, and Cole and Clay went inside while Flynn stayed behind to hold the button so the door would go all the way up. When he finally followed them inside, Cole already sat behind the wheel of the main tractor Flynn wanted to use.

He put the key in and twisted it, but nothing happened. Thankfully. Flynn didn't want to feel like an idiot in front of his friend and this mechanic.

"Could be a battery," Cole said.

"I bought and installed a new one," Flynn said. He had some skills.

Cole climbed down and opened the hood to look at the engine. "Some of these machines have safety switches," he said, bending over and digging around inside. He reached and grunted, taking several long seconds and lifting one leg all the way off the ground before he straightened.

"Okay, try it now."

Flynn climbed up into the tractor seat and turned the key. Miraculously, the engine sputtered and started. He couldn't believe it. Nothing he'd looked at online had mentioned anything about a safety switch inside the engine.

Cole moved to the next machine, but it didn't have a switch and still wouldn't start. "This one needs new spark plugs," he said. "I can get that done. Let's take a look at the next one."

One by one, he moved through the machines, getting three of them to start and diagnosing the others. He made notes in a small notepad, and then he and Clay left the farm to go to the farm supply store.

Flynn went inside and made grilled cheese sandwiches, feeling lighter than he had since moving onto the farm. With working machinery and cows, he felt like he knew what he was doing.

"Thank you, Lord," he whispered to the ceiling before he ate. When Clay and Cole got back, Flynn fed them and expressed his gratitude to them too.

"This place is so great," Clay said as they hung out in the shed while Cole worked. "Are you enjoying it?"

"Getting there," Flynn said with a smile. He looked at his friend. "Could you ask Jess to sit in for you at poker night?"

"She won't do it," Clay said. "She's already told all of us she's not available to sub." Clay sighed like he was the one losing something. "And I told her I'd arrange the transport of your cows if she'd tutor me the next time she came to poker night. She knew she'd never come to another poker night."

"Ever?"

"She loves you, man," Clay said.

Flynn didn't know what to say. He had to talk to Jess. Beg her to forgive him, and wait for him to figure things out at the farm. He'd spent a long time on his knees last night, and he was meant to be at this farm.

And he was meant to be with Jess.

So why couldn't he have both right now?

"How would you—what would you do?" Flynn asked.

"I have no idea," Clay said. "It took me six months to ask her sister out."

Flynn didn't want to admit how long he'd been watching Jess before saying anything. "How are things going with Cami?"

"Oh, we haven't been out yet," Clay said as the baler started up. "We're not going out for a couple of weeks. Cami's really busy around the ranch."

"You see her, though, right?" Flynn asked. "I mean, you don't have to go out to you know, see her."

"Yeah, I see her," Clay said, pushing off the workbench where they were talking. He threw Flynn a secretive smile and walked toward Cole.

Flynn watched the two of them work, and by the time they were ready to go, all the machinery was up and operational—at least for now.

"Call me if you need me," Cole said, and he and Clay left Flynn alone on the ranch again. He really didn't like to be alone, and his first instinct was to shower and get over to the dance hall. Plenty of women came out on Saturday nights, and Flynn wouldn't have to be alone.

He might actually have fun.

He stayed on the couch, too many thoughts streaming through his mind. He couldn't keep covering them up. Hiding them behind fake smiles and good dance moves.

His stomach grumbled, and he picked up his phone to order pizza. He had to pay a premium delivery fee to get them out to the farm, but he didn't care.

He then called Jess, desperate for her to answer. "Please pick up, Jess," he said, his plea becoming a prayer. "Please let her pick up."

CHAPTER FIFTEEN

Jessie woke when her phone rang. Light still streamed through her basement window, but it was waning and pure gold, meaning evening was definitely nearby.

She fumbled for her phone and picked it up. Flynn's name sat on the screen, and she hesitated. She had to decide quickly, or his call would go to voicemail, and she'd lose him again.

Emotion choked in her throat, and she looked away from the phone.

The device silenced, and her tears fell.

Call him back.

She shook her head against the thought, but it would not go away.

Call him back. Call him back!

Her phone started ringing again, and she winced. Flynn had called again.

Without getting too deep inside her head, Jessie slid open the call and lifted her phone to her ear. She couldn't speak, but she heard Flynn say, "Jess?"

Just the sound of his voice over a telephone line made everything inside her melt. She was so far in love with him, she couldn't see a way out.

She didn't want a way out.

"Are you there, sweetheart?" he asked. Something scuffled on the line, and he continued with, "Listen, I'm really sorry. I know I've been really busy here at the farm, and there's just been so many frustrating things, you know? I didn't mean to prioritize anything above you—above *us*—and I'm starving, and I just want to see you."

Jessie sucked in a breath, knowing he'd be able to hear it.

"I ordered pizza," he said. "If you left the ranch now, you'd arrive at the same time the food does. Please." He cleared his throat, his voice tight on the last word. "Please, Jess. I need you here with me."

"Why?" she managed to push out through her too-tight throat.

"Because I'm in love with you, and I can't stay at this farm without you."

His words rang through the line, through the bedroom, through her whole soul. "What?"

"I'm sure you heard me," he said. "But I'll say it again and again. I love you, and I love you, and I love you."

Jessie started laughing through her tears, the sound a little manic but also cheerful. She hadn't felt happiness in several weeks, and this emotion flowing through her just felt so good.

"I'll see you soon," she said, jumping to her feet. She looked around for her boots as Flynn said something, and she crammed her feet into them as she said, "Okay, Flynn. See you in a minute."

She grabbed her keys from her dresser and started for the stairs. Her nerves ricocheted all around her body as she drove, and she started weeping several times as she drove.

When she turned onto the dirt lane leading out to Four Lanterns Farm, she almost turned around.

Just keep going, she told herself.

Flynn stood from the bottom of the steps as she pulled up, and Jessie suddenly felt everything move into slow motion. She got out of her truck and tucked her hands in her back pockets, wanting to run to him but hesitant for some reason.

He jogged toward her, a smile playing across his face as he came. "Jess." He sighed, that smile so glorious. Pausing a few feet away, he looked at her. "I'm sorry," he said again. "I'm navigating some unknown territory for me, and I'm trying. I'm doing the best I can."

"I know," she said.

"I can't do this without you."

And judging by the way he hadn't shaved in a couple of days and the way he looked ready to drop on his feet, he really couldn't.

"I love you." He took a step closer to her. "Tell me you don't love me."

Jessie ducked her head, a smile cutting across her face. Light filled her being, chasing away the darkness of the last few weeks. "I love you, Flynn," she said, lifting her eyes to his. "I've loved you for a long time."

He gathered her into his arms, and the strength and security she found there was the greatest comfort she'd ever experienced.

"I got my tractors running," he whispered in her ear. "And the cattle are coming, and I think maybe things will start to settle down after the harvest."

"How are you going to harvest this place by yourself?"

"I'm not," he said. "Rhodes is bringing a crew, and I need you on it, Jess." He touched his lips to the top of her head. "I need you in everything."

"I need you too," she said, cradling his face in her hands. "So can you kiss me now, cowboy?"

"If you insist." Flynn touched his lips to hers, and happiness exploded through Jessie.

JESSIE HAD NEVER BEEN SO ITCHY OR SO HOT. SHE DIDN'T particularly enjoy the harvest, but having to do it twice? Finally, everything was finished on Flynn's farm, and everyone started heading into the homestead, where Flynn had ordered a catered taco bar from Ciran's taco truck. Jessie loved her cousins at the inn, and she had a pedicure scheduled with her sisters for Monday.

Anything to get relief from the extremely hard work over the past couple of weeks. At least the weatherman had said there would be cooler weather in the next couple of days.

She'd spent every evening with Flynn, and he'd even started coming by the hay barn in the mornings like he used to when he worked for Quinn Valley Ranch. He made time for her, and Jessie had enjoyed this autumn more than any other.

Except for the harvest times two, of course.

She entered his house as one of the last ones there, and the air-conditioning felt like a godsend. Glasses of water and lemonade sat on his kitchen counter, and she gulped one of them before refilling it.

"There you are," Flynn said, coming up beside her. He placed a kiss to her temple. "You hungry?"

"Starving," she said, leaning into his side.

"Eat," he said with a smile. "Everyone eat," he called louder.

Jessie enjoyed the time with all the cowboys at Flynn's house, and she had a flash of an image of the future right there in her mind. Eventually, everyone left, and Jessie snuggled into Flynn on his couch.

"Jess," he said, his voice tired and woozy.

"Yeah?"

"I don't want to be here without you," he said. "Will you marry me?"

Jessie sat up, surprise running through her. "Flynn."

"I'm serious, Jess," he said, smiling at her with his head back against the couch. "The sooner the better. Like, maybe tomorrow?"

"Tomorrow?" Jessie couldn't believe what she was hearing. "No. No, I can't marry you *tomorrow*. That's ridiculous." She half-laughed, half-scoffed, sure Flynn had maybe spiked the lemonade. Overdosed on tacos. Something.

"Soon, then," he said. "How long do you need to plan a wedding?"

"I don't—my sisters...." She shook her head. "Georgia is getting married the first week of November. Betsy is at Christmas. Rhodes and Capri just set a date in April."

"Let's tie the knot in January, then," Flynn said.

"We live in Idaho, Flynn. It's freezing in January.

"So you'll get a fur shawl," he said, smiling at her. He leaned forward, his dark brown eyes sparkling at the same time they sobered. "I mean it, Jess. I can't run this farm alone, and I don't want to wait for you to be mine forever."

"Well, I...I need to talk to Rhodes about what I do at Quinn Valley," she said. "I mean, I take care of the whole herd. I just can't—"

"Let's call him right now." Flynn reached for his phone, but Jessie put her hand on his.

"I'll work things out with my brother." She searched his face. "Are you really proposing to me right now?"

"Yes." Flynn grinned at her. "When we go visit my mother on Monday, we can stop at a jewelry store in Lewiston." He touched his mouth to hers in a quick kiss. "That's if you say yes."

"Well." Jessie didn't know what to say. She felt like someone had turned on a fan, and everything faded to white and then came back to full color.

"It's a simple question," Flynn teased.

Jessie searched his face again. She couldn't think of a single reason why she shouldn't say yes.

So she did.

"Yes."

Flynn chuckled, curled his fingers around the back of her neck, and kissed her. The very idea of becoming engaged right now with a wedding date only three months away was ridiculous. Utterly ridiculous.

She didn't care, because she was kissing her fiancé, the best birthday present she'd ever gotten.

Read on for a sneak peek of **FALL FIRESIDE** - **available in paperback!**

And keep reading to get the coveted Quinn family recipe for Granny's Sausage and Cheese Kolaches!

GRANNY'S SAUSAGE AND CHEESE KOLACHES

Granny's Sausage and Cheese Kolaches

$\mathcal{I}$NGREDIENTS

DOUGH:
 2 1/4 tsp yeast (One packet)
 1/4 cup lukewarm water
 1 cup lukewarm milk
 4 tbs butter, melted and cooled
 2 eggs
 1/2 cup sugar
 1 tsp salt
 4 3/4 cups flour (You may need up to 5 1/2 cups)

FILLING:
 12 fully cooked sausage links
 3/4 cup shredded cheddar cheese

1/2 cup jalapeño slices, optional

INSTRUCTIONS

1. In the bowl of your stand mixer (or whichever bowl you plan on mixing everything in), combine the yeast and water. Let rest to proof about 5 minutes.

2. With the mixer on low, add milk, butter, eggs, sugar, and salt until evenly combined.

3. Add 2 cups of flour and mix until blended. Add 2 more cups and mix until blended. Add the remaining 3/4 cup and continue mixing. If the dough still sticks to the side of the bowl, continue adding flour about 2 tbs at a time until the right consistency is reached.

4. Lightly grease the dough and cover with plastic wrap. Let rest at room temperature until the dough has doubled in size, about 90 minutes.

5. Meanwhile prepare a baking sheet by lining with parchment paper.

6. Punch down the dough and divide into 12 portions. Roll each into rectangles about 5 inch by 2 1/2 inch long.

7. Sprinkle 1 tbs cheese in a line down the middle. Layer on a few jalapeño slices, then lay on the sausage. Wrap the sausage in the dough, pinching to seal.

8. Transfer the kolache to the baking sheet, and place seam side down. Let rest for 30 minutes while the oven preheats to 350 F.

9. Bake until golden brown, about 25-30 minutes.

10. Let cool about 20 minutes before serving.

**RECIPE FROM WIDE OPEN EATS

Camille Quinn entered her sister's bedroom, her frustration reaching an all-time high. "Jess," she said, looking around, but her sister wasn't there.

She was probably out at Flynn's ranch, where she'd been spending more time lately. Cami flopped onto her bed, her tears not far behind. She sniffled, because she hated crying, and she wasn't going to let herself get out of control.

Not again.

Not over yet another cowboy.

Whistling met her ears before Jessie entered the room, and Cami glanced up. The whistling stopped, and Jessie said, "Oh, no. What happened?" She swooped to Cami's side, the way she always did.

"Gideon said he didn't want to go out with me again." Cami leaned into her sister's shoulder. "I just don't know what's wrong with me."

"Nothing's wrong with you," Jessie said.

"Why does this keep happening?" she asked.

"I don't know, Cami. You're cute. You're smart. You're funny. Maybe all these guys are just...losers." Jessie stroked

Cami's hair. "Granny just texted me. It was pretty unclear, because you know Granny and technology." Jessie chuckled, and Cami actually did too.

"But she has that peach delight we love, and I told her we'd come down since everyone else is off at the fair." Jessie stroked her hair back. "You want to? I mean, I know it's not a hot date on the Ferris wheel, but Granny and Gramps are pretty fun." She nudged Cami, who nodded.

"Yeah, all right." She got up and ran her hands through her hair. She normally didn't mind her natural curls, more brown than red, though the sun highlighted those auburn streaks. "Let me change first. I'm tired of wearing this belt."

"All right."

Cami could feel her sister's eyes on her as she rounded the corner and went further down the hall to the next bedroom, which was hers. She was much messier than Jessie, but she didn't care. And she didn't change right away either. In the past month or so, she'd been eating more potato chips—her favorite food—than normal, and maybe the belt was uncomfortable because she'd gained ten pounds.

Pushing the thought away, she changed quickly and ran upstairs to find Jessie chatting with someone on the phone, a smile filling her whole face. So she was talking to Flynn.

Cami paused and watched her sister, waiting for the jealousy to come. It didn't. Jessie had always been the sister on the sidelines while Cami went on date after date. Suddenly, she knew what that was like for Jessie, and regret filled her.

She entered the kitchen, and Jessie caught sight of her. She finished her call abruptly, and Cami hugged her. "Thank you for being the best sister ever."

"Oh, okay," Jessie said. She stepped back and held onto Cami's shoulders. "Why don't you go out with Clay? I know he asked you out, and you never went."

Cami didn't want to say why she'd told Clay that sure,

she'd love to go out, but then hadn't followed up with him. Harvest season had arrived, and Clay had been horribly busy, so he hadn't followed up either.

So she said, "I don't know," and hoped Jessie would let her leave it at that. She had a doubtful look in her eye, but she didn't say anything more. If there was someone who could text Clay and ask him what the heck he'd been thinking, it would be Jess. But Cami trusted her sister not to do that.

She worked on the family ranch too. She knew where to find Clay if she wanted to set up a date with him. She did... and she didn't. Her feelings were so very complicated right now, and she remained silent as she and her sister loaded up in Jessie's blue and white truck.

Jessie drove down the lane to Granny's, where they found Gramps sitting in a rocking chair on the front porch. "Gertie," he called as they got out of the truck. Cami's spirit lifted as she went up the steps to embrace her grandfather.

"Come see the turquoise eggs," he said, hugging the two girls at the same time. Gramps had just gotten several Ameraucanas, and he loved them more than anything at the moment.

"Oh, they don't have time to see your eggs," Granny said, coming out on the porch too. "Besides, I just got the peach delight out, and that's why they came." She kissed Jessie's cheek and then Cami's.

"I'll come see the eggs after we eat, Gramps, okay?" Cami said. She loved her grandparents, and she was glad she could see them often. Gramps loved ice cream more than any human alive, and when Cami needed a pick-me-up, all she had to do was get a carton out of the freezer and come down the road to the rocking chair on the front porch.

"Do we have ice cream to go with the peach delight?" Gramps asked, following the girls inside.

"Would it be peach delight without ice cream?" Granny

asked. Cami grinned and opened the drawer beside the fridge to get out the silverware. Jessie got down bowls, and Granny served the dessert.

Everyone moved over to the dining room table, where Granny had set out an old milk can filled with red, orange, and yellow flowers.

"All the fall colors," Cami said, beaming at Granny. Coming here had been exactly what her fragile heart needed. She'd never minded being the youngest, and she'd always known she'd be the last to find a fiancé and get married. Even though Jessie thought she'd be, Cami had always known she would be—and now she was.

"I'm thinking about getting new curtains," Granny said.

"Did you make these?" Cami asked.

"Yes, but they're having a bazaar at the church this weekend, and I'm thinking I'll get some there."

Cami met Jessie's eye, and they looked quickly away from one another. Cami smothered the giggles threatening to escape. She'd been set up by Granny loads of times before, and it seemed her grandmother's magic simply didn't work on Cami.

"There's that fireside series starting too," Gramps said.

"I'm not going to that," Cami said immediately.

"Why not, dear? It's a good series." Granny looked at her innocently. "We can go to the bazaar together, and then the first one on Saturday."

"Yeah," Jessie said, clearly enjoying herself. "I'm sure it'll be good."

"Are you going to go?" Cami asked, her eyebrows lifted high.

"Oh, I have plans with Flynn on Saturday night." Jessie beamed at Cami. "But you used to go to the fall firesides, every one of them."

"Yeah." Cami didn't want to explain that she'd first gone

because she was broken-hearted because of yet another disastrous relationship, and then to find a new date. Neither of those seemed like good reasons to attend a religious service, and she didn't want to admit them out loud.

"It'll be fun," Granny said. "And maybe you'll meet a man there."

"No thanks, Granny," Cami said. "I think I'm going to do what Flynn did. Thirty days. No dates. Male-fast."

Jessie made a strangled sound and shook her head. "Not a good idea, Cami."

"Why not?" She looked at her sister. "It's not like I have to follow it, but maybe I don't need to say yes to the very next person who asks me out."

"I really think you should try Clay," Jessie said.

Cami did like Clay, and she had been excited when he'd asked her out. But he must not have been as excited to go out with her, because it still hadn't happened.

"I'm texting him right now," Jessie said.

"You do that, and I will never speak to you again," Cami said.

"She's going to try her luck at the fireside," Granny said, and Cami watched as Jessie lowered her phone, a worried edge in her eye. Her sister had always looked out for her, and Cami glanced at Granny.

"Fine, Granny. I'll try my luck at the fireside." But she wasn't going to accept a date. Oh, no, she was not.

Granny's seventh attempt to set her up would fail again. But maybe the reverend would say something to soothe her ragged soul.

CAMI SMOOTHED DOWN THE MAXI DRESS, AS IT HID THE extra pounds she'd been packing on lately. She'd gone through her room and thrown out the bags of potato chips, and she'd been taking the stairs two or three times before breakfast to get in some extra steps.

It had only been three days since the peach delight with her grandparents, so it wasn't like she'd gotten rid of the weight she'd put on. Plus, she'd forgotten to look at the turquoise eggs that night, so she'd gone back last night with the banana ice cream her mother made and her excitement for colored chicken eggs at an all-time high.

The homestead felt so big these days, though her sisters all still lived here. But it wasn't the place it had used to be, full of chatter and laughter and weekend movies with flavored popcorn and too much soda.

Now, Betsy, Georgia, and Jessie spent weekends with their significant others, and for all three of them, that meant a fiancé. In fact, by April of next year—just seven months from now—all four of Cami's siblings would be married.

Maybe Granny *was* magical, as she'd been claiming responsibility for the success of her grandchildren's happiness, and not just in Cami's branch of the Quinn family. Cousins everywhere from the pub to the spa to the veterinary office had found love.

Cami sighed. She wasn't sure she wanted to start another relationship. Everything was new and exciting at first, but she worried she was shiny on the outside and completely dull on the inside. Once the men she'd gone out with rubbed off the gold, they were bored with her. Broke up with her. Or simply didn't call her back.

Or asked her out and then never set anything up.

She pushed the thoughts of Clay out of her mind. She had his number too. She could've texted him easily. In fact, she could've asked him what he was doing that night. Now that the harvest was over, maybe he'd have time to go to the fall fireside with her.

A faint horn sounded, and she gathered her skirts and hurried upstairs. Granny and Gramps sat in the truck, side-by-side, and Cami grinned at them as she skipped down the steps.

"Heya," she said.

"Are you ready for this?" Granny asked, a very proper hat on her head.

"So ready," Cami said, buckling her seatbelt.

"I think you'll meet someone tonight," Granny said. "I have a very good feeling about it."

"Okay, Granny." Cami laughed, and after a bumpy ride to the church, she climbed down and helped Granny out of the truck. They went into the church, the September evening air definitely holding a crispness to it that made Cami relax even further.

Autumn was her favorite season, and soon the leaves would be changing. Maybe when they came out of the fireside, fireflies would be buzzing in the air. Cami loved fireflies, but they didn't come to Idaho often.

"Did we get the time wrong?" Granny asked when they walked in. When she heard the choir singing, alarm pulled through Cami too. She went ahead of her grandparents to find that yes, the fireside was obviously already in progress.

And the chapel was very full.

Cowboy hats stretched from left to right, and Cami wondered if they'd be able to find a seat.

Her phone buzzed, and she lifted it up to see a message from Clay. Her heart skipped a beat, and she experienced a moment of believing she'd abandon her elderly grandparents here in favor of going out with him.

But he'd said, *There's space by me if you need a seat.*

She looked up to find one face turned back to her, an expectant smile on his face. "Over there, Granny," she whispered, pointing toward Clay.

As if they could miss him. The man stood up, and Cami was once again reminded of how handsome he was, how broad those shoulders were, how kind that smile as he ushered her grandparents onto the bench.

He looked at her, and Cami walked toward him, a grateful smile on her face. Or maybe it was a flirtatious smile. She wasn't sure.

What she was sure of was that she shouldn't have worn these heels, as one stuck on the long skirt of her maxi dress and she stumbled.

"Whoa," Clay said right out loud as he grabbed onto her. Cami felt the weight of dozens of eyes as Clay's strong arms kept her from falling all the way down.

A squeak came from her mouth as her fingers scrambled to find something to hold onto—and they found Clay's biceps.

Wow, he was strong.

Her mind blanked as she looked up into his dreamy eyes. "I got you," he said.

In the next moment, her face heated, and she struggled to get her balance back. She smoothed her hands down his arms and then up into her hair. "I'm okay."

Clay stepped out of the way so she could sit next to Granny, and Clay sat down beside Cami. There was not enough room for all of them, and she shifted closer to Granny while Clay lifted his arm around the back of the pew.

Warmth filled Cami, and a shiver ran across her shoulders from the nearness of him. So much for her swearing-off-men thing.

"Hey," he whispered, the heat from his body filling her and making her face flush. "You look great."

"Thank you," she whispered back, fighting the urge to lean into him as if she was his girlfriend. In the end, she gave up and let herself lean against him.

"Sorry we haven't been able to get together," he whispered. "Maybe I can make you lunch tomorrow after church?"

Cami turned toward him, and their faces were dangerously close. Close enough she could see the flecks of green in his blue eyes. Close enough to kiss him if she wanted to.

And oh, she wanted to.

You weren't going to say yes to the next man who asked you out, she told herself.

But she found herself saying, "Yeah, lunch would be great," before she faced the front and tried to focus on the pastor as he stood at the microphone and started his sermon. After all, it wasn't really a date if he was making lunch at his cabin. Was it?

"Great," Clay said. "We can sit together at church too, if you want. You drive with your sisters, right?"

She nodded, and Clay let his arm drop slightly so it was resting around her shoulders—just like a boyfriend would do.

And Cami didn't mind one little bit, even when Granny leaned over and whispered, "Isn't this an *amazing* fireside?"

You can read <u>FALL FIRESIDE</u>, the final book in the Quinn Valley Ranch series, in paperback right now!

Contracted Cowboy (Book 1): A fake ad brings a cowboy to Georgia's door just in time for all the Quinn family holiday parties, so she hires Logan to be her boyfriend. Nothing can go wrong with this plan...except she might lose her heart to her newly contracted cowboy.

Secret Sweetheart (Book 2): She's a domestic goddess. He works on her father's ranch. They could have forever...if they could take their relationship out of the shadows. **Can she overcome her anxiety and fear and build a life with Knox? Or will their relationship be doomed to die in the shadows at Quinn Valley Ranch?**

Landscaping Love (Book 3): He hired her to landscape the yard, but she's going to make him re-evaluate who he lets into his heart. **Can Rhodes and Capri landscape their love? Or will they go their separate ways once the yard is finished?**

Birthday Boyfriend (Book 4): This Quinn cowgirl doesn't need a lot for her birthday...just the cowboy she's been crushing on for months. Will Flynn ever see Jessie standing right in front of him?

Fall Fireside (Book 5): Cami Quinn has had enough of being the shiny new date for the cowboys in Quinn Valley. She's on her fifth or sixth broken heart, and she needs the soothing, healing messages she's found at the fall fireside series in the past. Will Cami and Clay find a way to mend what's broken inside themselves in order to find a happily-ever-after?

Liz Isaacson writes inspirational romance, usually set in Texas, or Wyoming, or anywhere else horses and cowboys exist. She lives in Utah, where she writes full-time, takes her two dogs to the park everyday, and eats a lot of veggies while writing. Find her on her website at feelgoodfictionbooks.com